Vengeance

Shara Azod

Copyright © 2015 Shara Azod

All rights reserved.

ISBN: 1517073685
ISBN-13: 9781517073688

Her scars ran so deep, her soul had been severed in two. Michelene had killed and run—but not far enough, or fast enough.

They'd found her.

Azriel had but one rule. No attachments. This rule had kept him alive. He'd lived by it—until her.

She'd found her savior in a man whose past was even darker than her own and whose soul held shadows of that dark. He made her body explode in ways she'd never imagined possible and gave her heart something she'd long given up... hope.

Michelene was his saving grace. The only thing which kept the darkness from consuming him. She was his to protect and cherish.

God help anyone who challenged that--because Vengeance would be his.

CONTENTS

1	Chapter 1	1
2	Chapter 2	Pg #11
3	Chapter 3	Pg #19
4	Chapter 4	Pg #30
5	Chapter 5	Pg #38
6	Chapter 6	Pg #47
7	Chapter 7	Pg #53
8	Chapter 8	Pg #62
9	Chapter 9	Pg #71
10	Chapter 10	Pg #75
11	Chapter 11	Pg #84
12	Chapter 12	Pg #92
13	Chapter 13	Pg #100
14	Chapter 14	Pg #105
15	Chapter 15	Pg #114
16	Chapter 16	Pg #123
17	Chapter 17	Pg #131
18	Chapter 18	Pg #139

Vengeance

19	Chapter 19	Pg #148
20	Chapter 20	Pg #160
21	Epilogue	Pg #167

All rights reserved. No part of this book may be used or reproduced electronically. All rights reserved. No part of this book may be used or reproduced electronically or in print without written permission, except in the case of brief quotations embodied in reviews. This is a work of fiction. All references to real places, people, or events are coincidental, and if not coincidental, are used fictitiously. All trademarks, service marks, registered trademarks, and registered service marks are the property of their respective owners and are used herein for identification purposes only.

© 2015 Shara Azod

Cover Art: Marteeka Karland
Editor: Katriena Knights

CHAPTER 1

Nice was just an illusion. Nice was the thing suburbanites liked to tell themselves they were, a pure delusion they needed to believe as they smiled and waved at their neighbors while secretly hating them, wanting to fuck their wives, wanting to live someone else's life, wanting to crush things they didn't understand.

Azriel wasn't into self-deception. He knew he wasn't a nice man—nowhere close to ever being one. Nor would he ever pretend to be anything other than what he was. On the best of days he was a bastard. Most other times—well, given his chosen profession, being a monster was an asset.

Psychologists could probably have a field day analyzing him, trying to get to the bottom of his particular psychosis. Had he been held enough as a baby? Did he have abandonment issues? Had his parents beaten him viciously?

It was all bullshit, really. He'd had a remarkably unremarkable childhood. Neither cuddled nor ignored, he was the miracle child of older, intellectual parents who spent a great deal of time teaching him, talking to him, showing him all the things parents are supposed to as well as a lot of things most kids are never taught until college. No one yelled at him, hit him, starved him. When they were alive, his parents were ideal. And while they were alive, they believed the same of him.

The truth was simple: Azriel was just different. He'd been good to his mother and father because that was what was expected. Anything outside the norm invited attention, and he made damn sure never to invite any kind of scrutiny. Never had he been moved to give a fuck about anyone other than Mr. and Mrs. Seth. Maybe he hadn't exactly felt love toward his parents, but certainly he was fond. He had to have been, as he cared enough to make sure their little world was never upset in any way.

But most of the swirling torment of emotions most people were subjected to seemed lacking in him. Frankly, he failed to comprehend why people bothered caring at all. It all seemed so very messy. He had no driving need to procreate. The very idea of children repulsed him. They were small, senseless and quite often a danger to themselves. Besides, why would he want a miniature person dependent on him for its very existence? His parents should be commended for keeping him; Azriel wasn't so sure he would've done the same in their place. Wants and needs that went beyond basic things made no sense to him. At least they didn't used to.

Until her.

For reasons he was extremely uncomfortable asking himself, Azriel was huddled in a dark corner in this shitty-ass neighborhood, waiting in the goddamn rain for a bus at one o'clock in the morning. He owned several cars, had a nice apartment uptown, a cottage up the coast—right on the beach—as well as various safe houses scattered about the globe. He wasn't on a job, wasn't scoping a potential job. There was nothing at all keeping him from being dry, out of this freak summer storm, sipping on a cognac or chugging a beer.

Nothing at all except her.

Grinding his teeth, he huddled back into the shadows as the city bus crawled to a stop. It was three minutes late, possibly because the driver had a severe drinking problem. The fact Azriel knew that pissed him off even more than he already was. There was no reason he should be researching anyone this thoroughly he wasn't planning on killing. But then, she emerged from the squeaking doors of the bus, wearing the butt-ugly mustard-colored polyester uniform, her hair pulled tight in a bun on the top of her head. His breath caught and held as she shot a frowning glance up to the sky, then hurried down the bus steps, attempting to tug the top of her uniform over her chest. Azriel allowed himself a little scoff. As if she could force the unyielding material over that magnificent cleavage. His mouth watered just thinking about the moisture that might be gathering on those deep brown mounds. Licking his lips, he forced himself back deeper into the shadows lest he be tempted to do something completely stupid.

Without sparing a glance to the right or left, she hurried down the sidewalk, those generous hips swaying even though he knew she wasn't trying to be provocative. With curves like that, she didn't have to try. The way she moved was innately sensual, no matter how hard she tried to look unassuming. She may have been walking fast, but she walked with complete unawareness of her surroundings. She probably had no idea she was being followed. That was the very reason Azriel was there, or so he liked to tell himself. The woman had managed to attract herself a stalker. Maybe Azriel would be here, following unseen even if there wasn't a predator watching her this very moment. Certainly he could've taken the guy out any time he wanted to, but he hadn't. Instead he just followed, watched, waited.

Azriel understood the attraction. There was just something about her—a sweetness that should've been stamped out of her long before now, yet hadn't been. Not once had he witnessed her ever fall victim to any of the vices so many residents of this part of time used to escape the horror of their existence. In a way, he was glad there was some sick freak out there stalking her. Otherwise, he would've been her stalker, and he didn't like to think about that. Knowing there was a man out there who would do her serious harm made Azriel her protector. It gave him a solid reason to follow her, investigate her life. As long as he had an excuse. Any other reason would mean some form of emotion, and that would greatly upset his philosophy of life.

There was him, and then there was everyone else—all potential prey.

Nothing else could be allowed in his well-ordered life. There was no loyalty in his business. Everyone he dealt with was in one way or another a criminal. A man would be a fool to ever trust a criminal. The man who paid him on Tuesday to get rid of one of his enemies could very well end up the man he was paid to kill on Friday. That was life. By that same token, no matter how good he was at his craft, there was someone out there just as good or better.

The man who paid him on Sunday would one day be the man who paid someone else to get rid of him on Monday. There was no room in his life for girlfriends, lovers, or even friends.

Careful to keep to the shadows, Azriel pushed such troubling thoughts away. Keeping his little bird in sight, he stealthily followed her through the pounding sheets of rain toward the dilapidated apartment building she called home. He would deal with the dilemma of this woman later. Maybe tomorrow he would kill her stalker and just be done with it.

Probably not though.

***

The mystery man was following her again. Michelene smiled at the secret knowledge her anonymous protector once again was walking her home. This made it the fourth night in a row. There was something about his presence that gave her comfort, especially since she'd acquired a certifiable stalker. The crazy man who cased her every move was out there too, but unlike her unseen protector, she knew the stalker wanted to hurt her.

There was no logical reason for Michelene to believe the first man only wanted to protect her. Other than a gut instinct, she had no way of knowing what was going on in the man's mind. Really, she had no real proof he existed at all, nothing other than a feeling. But she'd lived through enough to know she should always trust her instincts.

Since she was a child, her sixth sense had saved her over and over again. The few times she'd ignored that nagging inner voice, disaster had quickly followed. Against all odds, she knew he was there, and she knew he would never hurt her. Not in a bad way. But she also knew he was unsure of her. Moreover, he might be unsure of himself. There was a vibe she got every now and then, like he was confused why he was following her. Michelene wasn't confused. She knew, even if he didn't.

As for the real stalker… Shivering, she hastened her steps even more. There was proof the real stalker out there was a deranged son of a bitch who had fixated on her for some reason. The freak sent her emails with pictures of her at work, walking along the street, even buying tampons. How did he get her email address? How could he possibly know how many jobs she was forced to work? She used a different alias at each of her part-time positions.

Still, without fail, every month a box of chocolates appeared on her worn kitchen table on the first day of her period, which was beyond creepy. Flowers were left inside her apartment to mark the oddest anniversaries—the day she moved into this depressing neighborhood, the day she dropped out of the local junior college because she couldn't afford to go to school and pay rent at the same time, as well as the most disturbing date of all—the day she ran far from the only home she'd ever known.

No matter how bad things got for her on her own, she would never regret the day she stole away and landed here, in the lap of abject poverty. Every year for the past four years there had been a flowery card left on her pillow with just two sentences sprawled in barely legible writing. You are never alone. We'll be together soon. In her freaking bedroom! The freak had let himself inside and left her the card as if he were a lover.

What the heck did that even mean anyway? The police would do nothing because there was never proof he had been in her home, although she knew he had, and he had never approached her. Or maybe they just didn't want to be bothered. They had enough "real crime" in this area to deal with. Michelene couldn't have picked him out of a lineup if she tried; she'd never actually seen him. But he was out there. She was as sure of it as she was her protector was out there. And he was going to attack soon. Home invasions had become far more frequent. The sense of his growing malevolence was increasing. But when would he attack? More importantly, why her?

"Not tonight," she whispered to herself as she unlocked her front door. Tonight she had a guardian on her side. Tonight her protector was here.

***

She was too good for this place. Unlike so many of the women in this neighborhood, she didn't bring men to her apartment. She didn't tease down at the bars, or strip at the seedy clubs. And never, never was she on the corner selling what should be preserved only for the man she married. Michelene was a good girl, a clean girl. No matter what she called herself now, she would always be his little Michelene. An angel fallen from heaven. Soon he would help her back to her lofty home. They would go together, so they would never again be apart. She was perfection, true wife material.

And she would love him. She already did. He had proof! All his presents were kept in a box under her bed. Oh yes, he had been in her apartment many times. He knew what was in her refrigerator, and he knew there were no naughty toys in her drawers, no scandalous searches in her computer history. Plain cotton underwear and sensible, serviceable bras were all she wore under plain, bland clothing. Sweats or jeans, never dresses or skirts unless it was a uniform. Nothing too tight, nothing revealing. One day he would reward her for that. Buy her pretty things she could wear for him before it was time to leave this filthy planet. He would even allow her to continue reading the silly romance books she bought from time to time. All second-hand. His sensible girl.

Yes, she was perfect. She'd see he was perfect for her too. Just as soon as everything was ready, she'd see, and she'd understand why it had to be this way.

Soon.

CHAPTER 2

"I'm willing to pay you a lot of money to get this done. I need it finished this week."

Azriel popped his jaw, breathing in deeply to stem the tide of his rising anger. Yeah, Rico Cruz paid handsomely, but the man had an annoying habit of forgetting Azriel wasn't one of his flunkies. Doing two jobs for this guy was apparently two jobs too many. The encrypted email containing the details of the job Cruz wanted done hadn't been forwarded through a series of ghost routers from a dummy account until late last night. And this bastard wanted it done this week? That wasn't the way Azriel worked.

"Are you making demands?" Azriel purred low into the phone. Relaxing the death grip he had on the throwaway phone he'd used to call Cruz. If that had been Cruz's neck he would have snapped it without much effort. Drug dealers were the ultimate assholes. It was rare that he'd work for one; though admittedly he had when the mood caught him or other work was unappealing. One thing about his job—things were never dry. Although he'd had the encrypted emails redirected to the current burner phone he was using, he'd had no intention of accepting any of the job offers he currently scrolled through. The phone call to Cruz declining the job was mere courtesy as he had taken contracts from the man before. But never again.

"I'll be paying you more than enough to make fucking demands, *cabron*." Cruz either wasn't getting Azriel's point, or was deliberately ignoring the fact he wasn't going to get the hired gun he wanted for this job.

Okay, fine. Bluntness it would have to be.

"I am a free agent. I'm not on your payroll. I decide which jobs I will or will not take." And people like Cruz only hired outside help when they wanted no suspicion pointed their way from other crews or crime families. Tough shit for Cruz. "Keep your money. I'm busy."

"I'll triple your regular fee," Cruz pressed. Yet one more reason to avoid drug dealers. They really believed everyone could be bought, which meant they could be bought. They were the kinds of people who didn't blink an eye at selling someone out to save their own skin. "Name your price."

And now Azriel had a headache. He was almost tempted to take a quick trip to Bogota just because Cruz had succeeded in making his brain pound against his skull in an attempt to keep tight control of his temper. Since when the fuck did he have a temper?

"I'm. Booked." With that, he hung up, dropped the phone to the pavement and crushed it under his heel. After retrieving the SIM card, he scooped up the rest of the ruined phone, dropping it into the trashcan on the corner. The SIM card he kept, making a mental note to take care of it later.

The truth was he didn't have any jobs on the horizon because he refused to accept any. It would interfere with his current obsession—the woman who didn't belong. He didn't even know her fucking name, yet for some reason her safety—hell, just her being—had become his paramount concern. But why was she so damn important to him? What had started as a mere curiosity was growing to become something of an obsession.

How she came into his orbit had been completely coincidental. He'd been stalking a mark in this shitty part of the city, clocking the dude's movements. The client had wanted the guy disposed of in a way that looked like an accident, or natural causes. No small thing, as his target ran a smuggling ring—people and goods. The guy had bodyguards around him the majority of the time. The only constant in the man's routine was going to a diner for breakfast every morning. A greasy place that looked as if it belonged on some dusty road outside some tiny desert town. It was the only clear opening, so Azriel became a regular too. Generally waitresses in diners like that were uninterested at best. Tips tended to be sparse, customers rude and smelly, and the pay always sucked ass. It should've been easy to slip a drug that stopped the heart into his mark's coffee.

However she wasn't just any waitress. The woman always made sure her customers' coffees were fresh, mugs always filled, food brought out hot, the order always correct. And she was fucking vigilant. Far more than a dive waitress should be. She'd made it damn hard for him to get close enough to deliver the poison. The tag on her uniform at the diner declared her name to be Gladys, different from the hotel uniform name tag, which read Francis. Chances were excellent neither was her name. Especially as it took two or three times for her to answer when someone called her. Distracting her long enough to take care of his contract had taken far more effort than it should've taken. There was far more to the woman than met the eye.

Three nights ago, he'd convinced himself he was content to just watch her, protect her from the psycho stalking her if it came to it. But shit, who was he kidding? Of course he was going to have to take care of the stalker. And he wasn't sitting in this shitty diner in her section just because he felt a sudden urge to save a life instead of taking one. He was sitting here because he wanted to talk to her. Hell, he needed to hear her voice directed solely at him. Even more, he wanted to be seen by her. While trailing her to work this morning, he'd asked himself over and over again why he was doing this. There was no answer. There was no talking himself out of his current course of action, and he had no plan. That was not who Azriel Seth was.

There was some unseen force driving him toward her, and he found he couldn't turn away. He wasn't sure he even wanted to. That didn't mean he wasn't pissed at himself for even being here. No matter how much his logical side was telling him to get his ass up and as far away from this woman as possible he couldn't force his feet to move.

Azriel was going to take her, and he was going to keep her. Every fiber of his being screamed that this woman was his. And it was driving him crazy. Not once in his entire life had he ever felt the need for a personal relationship. Quite honestly, Azriel didn't like people in general. Sex was purchased at a price, generally high-end women who knew to leave as soon as the act was complete. He worked on his technique in case he needed it in the course of a job, which occasionally he did. Solitude was his mistress, silence the most beautiful symphony he ever heard. This was a disruption of his routine that he shouldn't be contemplating.

Yet…

"Good morning." The sweet, soothing voice he'd been waiting for sounded at his side. Deeper than he'd expected, but completely feminine. Somehow the woman had managed to catch him completely unaware. That never fucking happened. It could mean death not to be always on the alert. "Can I start you out with some coffee? I noticed you were still looking at the menu; I don't want to rush you."

His eyes might've been trained on the laminated paper in his hands, but he really hadn't been looking at anything. Another major no-no. He should've been aware of where every person in this diner was, which were the closest exits and the safest escape routes. Slowly he turned his gaze toward her, trying to brace himself. The last time he'd been this close to her, he'd been on a job. Although she'd captured his attention and held it at that time, he hadn't allowed himself to give much thought to his budding fascination with her then. He could now.

Too bad bracing himself wasn't enough. The full force of the impact on him up close and personal was—damn, he felt like he'd been shot in the gut at point-blank range.

Fucking breathe—shit, just breathe!

But sucking in air was suddenly a monumental task. Those lips! Lightly glossed. Thick and full, looking so goddamn delectable he wanted to nibble on them right then and there. Kissing them was more than a must; kissing them, biting that pouty bottom lip enough to make it sting. Those were the only lips that should ever be wrapped around his cock. And he wanted those deep-brown doe eyes staring up at him while she sucked him off. Those eyes should be glazed with satisfaction every fucking day of her life. There should be a secret smile behind them, and he should be their secret. His hands should be buried in that mass of riotous, tightly coiled, springy curls on the top of her head currently bound in a tight bun.

Great. Now he had a raging hard-on that wasn't going to go away anytime soon. Being this close had his mind full of visions of taking her every way known to man—and making up a few new ones. Yeah, coming into the diner had been a very, very bad idea. But it was too late now.

"Coffee is good." The only reason he spoke was because it would probably seem strange to her if he didn't. "And I'll have the special"—whatever the fuck that happened to be—"along with your real name."

CHAPTER 3

It was him! The guy who had been following her was sitting right in front of her. Not the creepy prey who left her weird "gifts," but her protector, the man who'd been keeping her safe. Funny—in her head her mystery man hadn't been attractive at all. Not in the conventional sense. She'd always imagined he looked similar to a human beast, all fierce and scary.

Michelene had apparently been very, very wrong. Yes, this man was scary looking, but he was also beautiful. No, he was beyond even that. He was magnificently elegant, so out of place in such drab surroundings. Sitting in the worn vinyl booth in a suit and tie that looked tailored, with the rising sun shining directly behind his head, he looked almost otherworldly. Thick, dark hair, cut brutally short, graced his perfectly shaped head. The haircut didn't hide the promise of curls. The mouth was cruel, but looked so sinfully sensual. The kind of lips that new how to bring a woman ultimate pleasure. Chiseled featured looked as if they were made of stone, then encased in warm flesh. But it was his eyes that got her. Cold gray eyes regarded her in an unblinking stare as if he was waiting for her to admit she knew who he was.

Did she just think his eyes were cold? No, that wasn't right. They were icy hot. His stare burned her, kept her rooted to the spot. Despite those insanely thick, long, black lashes, this man was the epitome of all that was masculine. A true male in heat. And he had branded her as his own for some reason. Oddly, she was perfectly okay with that. More than okay. Her body reacted as if he had just announced he was here to take her home—a thing she hadn't had in so very long. All those dense, packed muscles would keep her safe. Finally.

Wait—no, this was insane. Her fanciful daydreams were getting the better of her again. Michelene blinked, stepping back a little. As soon as she did so, his gaze dropped to her feet, which immediately made her return to the spot where she'd been originally standing. The action was as innate as it was immediate, and she could've kicked herself for it. Only, he smiled. A crooked grin that was really more of a wry twist of lips. But to her, it was as if the full force of his approval beamed a special light just for her. She actually preened a little.

God, she really needed to get a grip!

"Why don't you have a seat and join me for a little while?" her protector asked in a voice so deep, the timbre seemed to drum right through her, landing in her bones and making her vibrate from the inside out.

"Gladys! Get that sweet ass of yours in gear!" Vic, the diner's manager/cook bellowed through the wide opening between the kitchen and the counter. "You ain't getting paid to gab! If the guys doesn't know what he wants move the fuck on and come back later. There's paying customers waiting on you!"

There wasn't time to cringe. In a split second, she saw something flash in her mystery man's eyes—something dark and deadly. Sensing he was about to move, her hand shot to his shoulder, her heart pounding as she tried to communicate her desperate plea with her eyes. "Please don't.

The panic that was squeezing her throat wasn't because she was afraid for Vic; she could care less about that greasy pig. Nor was she concerned this man could be hurt. She knew she couldn't afford scrutiny. She'd managed to be virtually unseen for four years; it had to remain that way. It was amazing this man didn't know who she was. "Vic's an ass, but he's harmless." Her words weren't moving him in the least. There was no visible change in his manner, but Michelene sensed he was growing more pissed, more dangerous. "He's never laid a hand on me."

That worked. She felt his tension drain a bit, while he stared pointedly at where her hand rested on him. She didn't move it. Slowly, he turned those ghostly eyes back to her face. "If he talks to you like that again, I will end him."

Would most women feel the same thrill she did at his words? Not having much experience with "normal" people, Michelene really couldn't say. But she certainly felt thrilled right down to her toes. Pussy clenching, she knew she needed to put a little space between them before she did something that would garner even more attention. Before it came to that, she tried to move, but found her arm caught in a vise made of hot flesh.

"Your name," he growled, his piercing glare keeping her rooted to the spot every bit as much as his hold.

"Michelene," she whispered back, not even considering giving him a fake name. Besides, she was sick of not being herself. There was something about him, a danger, a certain "off-ness" that called to her, told her she could be herself around him.

"Nice to meet you, Michelene." There went that smile

again. Just that tiny sign of approval succeeded in melting her formerly icy insides. "I'm Azriel Seth."

"I'll bring you your coffee, Mr. Seth."

Scurrying to the counter before she fell flat on her face, she had to brace herself on the formica, taking deep gulping breaths to try to calm herself enough to actually pour the coffee. Azriel Seth. The freakin' archangel of death. If that was the name he'd been born with, his parents must've been psychic or something. There was no doubt in her mind Azriel could've ended Vic if she hadn't stopped him. That she had managed to stop him was a minor miracle in itself.

Knowing who he was should've horrified her. Instead her panties dampened, her nipples rock hard as she attempted to pretend she didn't feel this instant, irresistible pull toward him. Yeah, the guy was undeniably sexy, blessed with a face that was breathtakingly handsome accentuated by one of those deep, dark, sensual voices, but he was way outside her league. Hell, she didn't even have a league. Normal dating was impossible for her. Had always been a non-starter. She wouldn't know what to do with someone like him.

All this time, she had been shadowed, protected by the angel of death himself. Of course she knew exactly who he was, heard whispers of all he'd done. Holy fuck, she'd given him her real name! What the hell had possessed her to do that? Just because he'd asked her, she'd immediately responded like some kind of wind-up doll. And it had felt good! Lying to him just seemed...wrong. Even though it was only her first name, it was way too much information for a man in his profession. For all she knew there could be a hit out on her; in fact, she wouldn't be at all surprised. Staying low, living in the worst conditions had kept her secret this long. No one would ever think to look for her in the slums of the same city that had always been her primary home.

"Hey Gladys, why don't you let me help you out?" Genie, the artificial redhead and perpetual pain in her ass gave her a huge Cheshire cat grin. Right. Help her out. This ought to be rich—the only time Genie ever lifted a finger was when it was to her benefit, or to pull a trick. Michelene had to admit, it took balls to prostitute on the day job in between carrying food out to the masses.

"How's that?" Michelene asked, busying herself with Azriel's coffee.

"I'll take that coffee over to twelve for you." Giving Michelene what she guessed was supposed to be a friendly smile, Genie all but snatched the coffee off the counter. "In fact, why don't I just take the table for you altogether?"

Of course. Azriel was the only guy in the diner who looked like he wasn't some low-level criminal or a wage slave. Poor Genie. Little did she know he was actually one of the best hit men in the business. It was on the tip of Michelene's tongue to tell the overused hooker to go fuck herself, but she stopped. If Michelene went back over there, she was liable to do something even more stupid than she already had. Like confessing the reasons she was here working shitty jobs for shitty pay, living in squalor.

Plus, the woman in her that she'd never allowed out really wanted to test him. What would he do when hit on by Genie? Not by any stretch of the imagination did Michelene believe Genie had a chance in hell, but she wanted to watch.

"Sure." Gracing the bimbo with the biggest, brightest, fakest smile she could manage, Michelene took a step back. "Have at it. One less table for me."

Although she made like she was busy, which she was, she couldn't resist watching covertly as Genie approached Azriel with an exaggerated swing of her narrow hips. Honestly Michelene didn't have a clue what might happen, but this was giving her valuable time to try to get herself together. That fierce scowl he proffered was kinda funny. But then he got to his feet and began to stalk in Michelene's direction.

Oops. Maybe this wasn't such a good idea after all. Man, he was pissed. On his face there may have been zero emotion, but she could actually feel the anger coming off him in hot waves. Why the hell was she so in tune with this man, this cold-blooded killer?

"Hey!" Poor, stupid Genie just wasn't used to customers ignoring her. Too bad she failed to recognize Azriel didn't belong here. You don't belong here, either, a nagging voice inside her whispered. Put Michelene pushed it away. Something told her she wouldn't be here for long now anyway. Might as well enjoy the show.

When Azriel ignored Genie, the idiot reached out to grab his arm. Michelene damn near swallowed her tongue as Azriel stopped cold, a tic evident in his jaw. The way he looked at Genie's hand was completely different from the way he'd looked at hers. If she were Genie, she would've beat feet. Genie wasn't the sharpest tool in the shed, however.

"You can't seriously prefer some chubby nobody over me!"

Wow, until now, Michelene'd had no idea how seriously deluded Genie was. They'd always been cordial more or less, but that was just—wow. Michelene knew she might not be drop-dead gorgeous, but she looked a damn sight better than an aging whore who didn't even try for better. And yeah, she wasn't rail-thin, but real women had curves. Unlike Genie, she'd never had need for surgical help to fill her bra cups. Paying for implants while living and working in the worst part of town was beyond stupid. That money could have been used to learn a real trade.

"You think your well-used, dubious charms are anywhere near as worthy as Gladys's natural beauty?" Azriel's voice may have been low and even, but it could be heard clearly throughout the diner. Every conversation had ceased. It wasn't every day a man dressed like Azriel, whose slacks and shirt cost more they made in a month, came to eat among them. It was even rarer any man ever said no to Genie, and so publicly too. All eyes were trained on the little mini-drama, with Genie looking confused and hurt and Azriel looking…unflappable. People here weren't as stupid in general as Genie. One look told a person everything they needed to know about Azriel. The man moved like he was bringing death in his wake.

"I-I am better." Only Genie didn't look as convinced as she sounded. Come to think of it, she didn't really sound all that sure anymore, either.

"You are a low-class streetwalker past her prime." Azriel spoke dispassionately, as if he were observing her as a scientist might. And he wasn't done. "Your soul is black, your prospects non-existent because you've killed them all, and your life expectancy continues to decrease with every john you manage to con to make free use of your body. I am also willing to bet you carry more than one nasty surprise for any fool dumb enough to suck you. You repulse me."

Well, damn. Genie's hand fell away like the appendage was nothing more than dead weight. The words were harsh, cruel even, but Michelene was more than a little turned on that this man saw through the surface and got right down to the heart of the matter. How many times had she been left to serve Genie's tables while she turned tricks in the bathroom or outside in the alley? And Vic let her as long as he got a cut. Not only did he allow it on her shift, but he fed her ass when she wasn't working so she could hang around the diner trolling for johns. Michelene had actually had to wait on her too many times. Genie had never been overtly nasty, but she was dismissive, uncaring who suffered as long as she got her way. And she had always been far too full of herself.

Now Genie turned every shade of the rainbow, running from the dining area to stumble through the swinging door leading to the kitchen. Michelene knew a normal person might feel a little sorry for the woman. She just didn't have it in her. Genie was a bottom feeder—something like this was probably long overdue.

As for Azriel, he didn't spare the other waitress another thought. He finished stalking over to her, stopping in her personal space. He said nothing, but those eyes—fuck, she was in trouble. Whatever he was planning, she was down. Didn't even matter what it was, she was already down. The fact her very life could well be on the line didn't matter.

No, that mattered, but she was sure her life was safer in his hands than anywhere else. If she kept hiding here, she would die here without living at all.

"Gladys! What the hell did you do to Genie! You better move that big ass. You're covering all her tables, goddamn it!" Vic went full bellow from the pick-up window.

The tic returned to Azriel's jaw. Please don't kill him, she silently prayed, but didn't dare ask.

"She quits," Azriel bellowed right back, causing her to jump. He never looked away from her, and ignored the string of threatening curses coming from Vic at his statement. "The only reason I am allowing that man to continue breathing is because it would upset you if I killed him here and now. Consider this a gift. Now you are coming with me."

Michelene didn't say a word because there was nothing else to say. She was going with him.

CHAPTER 4

What was she doing? Why was his angel leaving with that man—that animal? Azriel Seth was the devil incarnate. Oh, yes, he knew who that butcher was. But Michelene didn't. She couldn't possibly. His angel was a sensible girl. She was pure, innocent. He had watched over her; he knew that, despite the filth she'd grown up in, she had managed to remain unaffected. For years he had watched and waited, knowing she was the one for him. His unblemished bride. The dregs of humanity might have borne her, fostered her, but she was heavenly to him. Hadn't she run from those who would've corrupted her? And now she was leaving with a demon of a man?

No, it couldn't be. But his eyes weren't lying to him. Not this time. They sometimes lied, but he had mastered those lies. He was in control in a way he hadn't been in years. All because of her. Because it was almost time for them to be together. Surely this development was Satan trying to keep two celestial beings apart.

Azriel had his arm around Michelene's waist, walking her away from the diner, away from her adopted neighborhood. Of course the bastard would have a car stashed close somewhere nearby. He followed them to a parking lot just outside the seediest part of town, where Michelene had made her home. The lot had security, the real twenty-four-hour kind that did rounds around the lot and carried real guns. There was no way he could get close, no way he could stop this kidnapping. Azriel marched the woman who was his and his alone to a sleek black Jaguar. Such displays were ungodly, obscene. Right before his very eyes, the beast lifted Michelene's chin with two fingers, leaned down and—

NO! Oh, God no! This couldn't be happening. That gutter swine put his lips on his woman, his pure angel! Big, beefy arms engulfed her, pulling her tight against his frame. That man was unclean! He was defiling her!

The world was spinning; he couldn't breathe. A haze of foggy red mist clouded his eyes so much he couldn't see clearly. At least he could no longer focus on what Seth was doing to his beautiful Michelene. It wasn't much of a blessing, as the spinning was getting progressively worse, making it impossible to stay on his feet. As the unforgiving sidewalk slammed into his knees, he heard the distinctive sound of the smooth purr of the luxury engine coming to life, heard the car's slow roll to the gate before gaining speed as it no doubt disappeared down the street. In no time, his angel would be swallowed into morning traffic, disappearing among hundreds of metal boxes on wheels. There was no way he could know which direction.

HIs chest constricted painfully, pain piercing his skull. The pounding of his brain against the solid bone was excruciating. He was going to lose his angel. How could this be happening? He couldn't lose her now. Michelene was his hope, his future. They were meant to ascend together as one. So close; he'd been so very close. Seth would only defile her, mar her. Damn it, her purity belonged to him, not that monster!

"I'll find you," he whispered to the wind as the pitch black of nothingness reached out to embrace him. "I'll find you and I will purify you."

Someway, somehow, she would hear him and take heart. He knew she couldn't have gone with that man intentionally. She'd been tricked. That was the only way she would've gone with him. For too many years he had watched and waited; he couldn't give up now. Not now, not ever.

***

Yeah, he'd been pissed by the skank back at the diner. Stomping down the street with Michelene in tow, Azriel gritted his teeth, wanting nothing more than to eradicate the diner from the face of the earth. It was laughable that the slattern had believed herself to be more desirable than Michelene. Why the hell would he ever want someone who was so obviously well used compared to a woman who was as fresh as spring's first blooms? Azriel could smell a pro at fifty paces; that the woman had approached him like she was honestly interested in more than a transaction was fucking offensive. He wasn't a wet-behind-the-ears boy, and he'd had his fair share of call girls. He didn't judge, but he wouldn't be played. He had a healthy respect for women who were forthright with what they wanted. Given the diner's usual clientele, he could fully understand a working girl wanting a john with a big fat wallet. Azriel was the last one to begrudge the hustle; hell, everyone had to hustle once in a while. Only he was no one's mark. And the woman had dared to place her hands on him…

While his parents were alive, Azriel had kept up the pretense of having relationships with women, when really, he didn't understand the attraction. From the time his parents died up until today, every sexual experience had been with professionals, though ones of a much higher caliber than the woman from the diner. Conversations, going places, pretending to care had always been tedious to him. All the while he was usually thinking of anything else. Planning an assignation in a backward third-world country ruled by a paranoid tyrant was less taxing.

Then came Michelene. It was like the universe had waited to dump a shit load of caring into this tiny, curvaceous package. He was caring too much, about every part of her life, and that just wasn't how he was.

Fury had blazed when both the fat cook and the skinny hooker had demeaned her. God, how he wanted to wrap his hands around each of their necks! Anyone insulting her, anyone yelling at her as if they were better than her— it couldn't be allowed to stand. He was going to have to go back there. Otherwise that fat, sweaty man might think he had a right to yell at Michelene. And the waitress… He would think of something. Her audacity at believing herself to be better than Michelene was bad enough. He had to wonder what her cruel words had done to the woman he had taken an obsessive interest in.

If he cared to be honest, he would have to admit some of his anger stemmed from the fact that he was so interested in this woman. He was pissed that she needed him to protect her. Pissed that she worked a series of shitty jobs from the crack of dawn to well after nightfall just to make ends meet. And she didn't fucking belong in that neighborhood. She hadn't grown up there, but she managed to fit in as if she had. That was worrisome. But not so much so he wasn't taking her to one of his homes now. And it should've given him enough pause to never risk what he was doing now.

"I can't walk as fast as you can. I need to slow down."

The clear, sweet feminine voice held no coquettishness, no artifice. Just a simple statement of fact. Azriel slowed his steps immediately. Thankfully, they were approaching the parking lot where he'd left his car while watching over her. Located just outside her neighborhood, it offered twenty-four-hour roaming security camera surveillance and easy, quick access to the freeway.

"We're here," he found himself uttering unnecessarily as they stopped right next to his Jag. Until that moment he'd had no real explanation why he chose to drive this car here during the early hours before he knew she left her first job. Generally he would drive a dark blue or gray compact car when surveilling anyone. They were harder for anyone to identify or even remember. Just like generally he would've dressed down for days when he planned on interacting, wearing cheap jeans and a cheaper shirt, cheap shoes, maybe a baseball cap. Today he was in high-end wear from top to bottom. For her—he did this all to impress her. On some level he'd known he would be taking her with him today. He just hadn't wanted to admit it.

And she hadn't so much as batted an eyelash. Even now, standing right next to his Jag, she didn't even glance at the car. He wasn't foolish enough to think she didn't know what it was. She just wasn't impressed. Or even surprised. Looking him straight in the eye, she waited for him to make a move, nothing but patience in her gaze.

Aww, hell!

Kissing those full, pouty lips was his only option. So that was exactly what he did and…

Sweet holy fuck, her lips were soft! He'd meant to take them forcefully, to exert his dominance. But as soon as his lips touched hers, all he could think about was getting a deeper, fuller taste. Slanting his head, he did just that, sliding his tongue inside her mouth. God, he just wanted to push her up against the car, rip off her panties and bury his bare cock so far inside her that he could lick his own tip with his tongue in her mouth. That was going to have to wait because he'd be damned if he would do that here. Just because the taste a public fucking would afford him wouldn't be nearly enough.

Because her hair was caught up in a tight, unforgiving bun, he couldn't spear his hands through the tight coils of her natural curls. Instead, his hand held her by the neck, forcing her to tilt backward. It gave him deeper access to her mouth, which was equal parts heaven and hell. Fuck, he just wanted her in the worst way. He had to keep his other hand tight against his own side or else he would probably rip that ugly-ass uniform off what he knew to be a gorgeous body.

Home. He needed to get her home. Somewhere far away from here, far away from whoever was following her, away from the shitty-ass apartment she used to live in, away from the crappy jobs. All that rage he'd felt earlier had transformed into something else, something far more urgent. Now all he felt was lust. His entire being was one giant ball of need. There wasn't a thing on him that didn't throb with the urgency to mark her, make her his.

"Get in," he growled, clicking the automatic lock and opening the door for her in one smooth move. "I am taking you home."

CHAPTER 5

I am taking you home.

A lump formed in Michelene's throat when she heard those words in that deliciously dark snarl. They made her want to cry. However, she didn't dare. She sensed that would probably freak him out. Still, his words washed over her like a gentle wave propelling her to safe harbor—finally. Sure, she was aware he simply meant he was taking her to his home. But she was also aware there was meaning in the fact he didn't specify that. Men like Azriel tended to be very careful with their words. The slip couldn't have possibly been unintentional, but he still was saying a lot.

Finally, after four long years, she was going somewhere she could let her guard down, somewhere she would be completely protected. Maybe even cherished, if the look in his eyes were to be believed, and Michelene was choosing to believe.

So she got in the car. There was no need to ask where they were going because it didn't matter. When she'd run from home so long ago, she hadn't had a plan. Never in a million years had she dared to dream she'd be rescued. At least not by a stranger—a sexy, enigmatic stranger who would kill someone for merely annoying her.

Keeping her head down, she'd worked, even tried to go to school. The school part hadn't worked out so well. But she hadn't given up and done something stupid that would've gotten her caught. Instead she just kept slogging on day and night, saving what tiny bit she could in hopes one day she would be able to really escape. Far away where there was no chance of being caught.

That too hadn't been working out so well. She'd never known how hard it was for the average person to scratch up enough money just to survive. Time had been running out; she knew that when she had caught the eye of whoever else had been stalking her.

But then she'd felt Azriel's presence. Only then had she known it would be okay. Honestly, she'd expected one of the smarter neighborhood goons to recognize her long before now. Then it would've been over. How close she had been to just giving up. Then there he was—her very own angel haunting her every step. Making sure she was safe.

As far as Michelene was concerned, they had already had a courtship, though not a conventional one. There didn't need to be flowers, movies or dinners. She would give Azriel whatever he asked for, because he would give her everything. Funny how he didn't even know that yet, but he would. Being with her would be a test, but she had a feeling he wouldn't bat an eyelash. This was no knight in shining armor—they both knew that. Those kind of men just didn't exist in her world. There was no way she would've survived this long without recognizing the wolf inside the man. She'd grown up around such types; she knew what they preyed on. Only Azriel was far more dangerous than anyone she'd ever met, and that was perfect in her eyes. Thrilling, even. This was the wolf that hunted other wolves. The perfect hunter. Another woman would be wise to be terrified. But not her. Especially not after that kiss.

When his body had been so tantalizingly close to hers, she felt the barely suppressed violence in him. Like he couldn't decide whether to kill her or fuck her right there. But she knew he wouldn't hurt her.

"You should be scared." As if he could read her thoughts, he succinctly expressed what she was feeling.

A serene smile that started deep in her core radiated

outward long before it showed on her lips. She didn't answer because it wasn't a question. Watching as he sped through the crowded streets, zipping in and out of lanes as if he couldn't get to his destination fast enough, Michelene took the time to study him covertly. He was bold, she'd give him that. Completely unafraid of being stopped. In so much of a hurry to get her alone. That was the best turn-on ever. Knowing she was driving this urgency in him was making her wetter than she already was. Not to mention the rough beauty of his him—all of him. He looked like a cardinal sin, one she was going to love committing.

God, how she burned watching that tic in his jaw. That seemed to be his only tell; she noticed it back in the diner. The way his eyes narrowed as he navigated, pushing the car as fast as traffic would allow, caused her nipples to tighten painfully. Would his hands grip her as hard as he was gripping the steering wheel? Would his eyes have that burning glow as he watched her undress? Would he even be patient enough to allow her to? God, her panties grew even wetter at the prospect. Sexual frustration was emanating from him in waves, filling the vehicle and wrapping all around her body. It was hard not to rip off her clothes right then and there.

"You haven't asked where I'm taking you." Azriel turned that eerie gaze on her for a few heartbeats before turning back to the road. The tic in his jaw began to pulsate in earnest. It was cute that he was irritated by her acceptance. Like he would've accepted anything less. "Why?"

"Because it doesn't matter." What was she supposed to do, complain if she didn't approve of the location? Their entire situation was so far outside the norm, such concerns were completely out of place. "There's a lot of question should've asked me too, but you didn't. Like my last name, for instance." Because that answer could make all the difference in the world.

"It doesn't matter who you were," he growled back without missing a beat. "You are mine now."

***

"M-m-Madam Brown, I, uh, know you were, um, you are looking for the girl..." Madam Bitch was more apt. Stupid cow shouldn't be allowed to breathe, much less make him stutter like a callow youth. It galled him to have to come to her. If there had been any other way... If only his cousin would've agreed to help. But no—he had been forced on this course of action before his cousin would lift a finger. Why was a mystery.

The things he went through for his angel! He'd thought he'd lost Michelene forever, thereby losing his only salvation. But fate had brought her back to him. He was convinced it was divine intervention. There was no way he was letting her out of his sight now. So he would swallow his pride and prostrate himself before this Jezebel, this Whore of Babylon. In the end, he would have heaven and together they could vanquish this beast of a woman.

She was older than she looked, this creature in front of him. Sitting on a carved wooden chair meant to imitate a throne, she was flocked by two muscle-bound dunderheads. He could have sworn he recognized one of them, but it was difficult to see clearly. His head still ached when he thought of his angel in the hands of Azriel Seth. Another demon who needed to be disposed of.

"I know where she is—was." It was so hard to keep up the facade of being afraid, subservient. "I know where she's been until earlier today."

The woman simply raised an artificial brow, not speaking. The painted, blood-red lips thinned just a bit though. Ahhh, she was interested. He was willing to bet inside she was clamoring for the information he held. But the bitch had to keep up appearances, didn't she? Well, he could play this game too. Closing his mouth, he waited, knowing his silence was driving her crazier by the second. It was petty, but the hatred he had for this woman knew no bounds. She was pure evil; nothing more than the pus seeping from an infected wound. Any way he could make her suffer was a plus. Like staring at the five-strand pearl necklace around her throat. Oh, yes, he knew why she wore it. Did her neck ache a little? God, he prayed so.

"If you know where she is spit it out," Madam Brown snapped, a deep frown suddenly marring her face. It gave window to her true age. "Where's she been won't help, idiot. She's too smart to leave clues." Her last sentence held a little pride. That was curious.

"The apartment she's been living in is untouched, all her things still there," he announced smugly, hoping that was still true. "She was taken—she didn't leave voluntarily." That he needed to believe. Desperately.

"Who would dare take her and not bring her to me? I have a fucking bounty out on her pretty little head!" Now Madam Brown was on her feet, snarling as she stomped toward him. Nails painted the same blood color as her lips curled into claws as she reached out to grab him around the neck. There was spittle in the corners of her mouth, her nostrils flaring. "Who? No one has approached me!"

"Seth," he choked out, thankful for the physical assault. It hid his glee. All he had to do was offer to bring his angel to her, and he could find out where Seth had taken her. "Azriel Seth."

"The angel of death?" Madam Brown actually stumbled back, releasing him entirely. How lovely it would've been to watch her fall on her ass. Too bad one of her flunkies stepped up to catch her. "Out! Get out!"

Shit! This wasn't the way it was supposed to go!

"I can bring her to you," he blurted out, his game plan falling apart in front of his eyes. "I just need a little help finding Seth—"

"And you think I know where he is? Get the fuck out before I forget what you once did for me," she raged, her face so contorted there was none of the beauty he'd noticed before left in her visage. This was the real Maylene Brown. Ugly to her bones.

As much as he wanted to push, he knew better. The woman had no real loyalty to anything, not even her own word. Defeated, he turned to leave, one of her goons trailing behind him.

Only, once they were out of earshot of the others, the man stopped him.

"Your cousin said once you have delivered the news about the girl, I'm to tell you Seth has a place up the coast, outside of Cayucos." The goon took a quick look over his shoulder, then lowered his voice even more. "The place is isolated, but bound to have heavy security. You are only to take the girl and make sure she is never seen or heard from again."

Yes! He knew his cousin wouldn't fail him! Hurrying

on his way, he began to make his plans. No one could stop him now; Michelene would finally be his. It was just a matter of time.

CHAPTER 6

Azriel had every intention of taking Michelene to his beach house. It was both secluded and beautiful, a perfect place for him to get to know this woman thoroughly. At least, he'd intended it when he had first started to march her toward his car. Before that, he hadn't really planned on anything at all, which was completely out of character for him. When it came to this woman, nothing about his actions were rational or within his usual routine. It was fucking unnerving. This morning he'd only set out to continue his surveillance. After a sleepless night bombarded by a craving so deep it made him shake, one he failed to understand, he'd decided to kill the thin, sickly guy who'd been following her and move on. It would've been the ideal solution aside from killing her.

Gone was the irritation he'd experienced waking up to

a rigid cock in his hand, the final vestiges of her ghost fading with the dawn. Since fucking when did he masturbate? Let alone in his sleep? Azriel didn't dream. Not ever. Why was this woman invading his rest? Yet, despite his determination to end this obsession, he'd seen her and all those things he'd planned to do vanished. One look and he knew this was never going to end for him. She would always be on his mind. So he took her.

There wouldn't be the long drive to his beach house. As much as he hated to admit it, he couldn't last that long without feeling her skin, kissing those fucking addictive lips. As it was, his cock throbbed so hard it hurt, aching to be inside her. Another in a long line of firsts. Kissing her so soon had been a serious misstep. The need to taste her more deeply rode him hard.

His uptown apartment would have to do. The security was stellar, though not as intricate as at the beach house, but that was okay. Other than her stalker, who would give a shit he had taken her? As far as he could tell she had no one. Well, before now she'd had no one. Instinct still had him taking the back entrance to the high rise. The valet would've been faster, and speed was of the essence, yet he couldn't shake the need to keep her his little secret. His determination didn't supersede his requirement for privacy.

Haphazardly parking his car as close to the elevator as he could, he hustled her out of the vehicle and onto the polished stainless steel lift with more force than he'd intended. But not so much that he'd apologize. After stuffing the key into the lock that would allow the elevator to take them to the top floor, he whirled on her, pushing her against the gleaming surface of the back wall. How small she seemed against his admittedly much larger than average frame. The top of her head barely cleared the bottom of his chest. Petite she might be, but that body was nothing short of lush. Like a pagan fertility goddess, she was built to carry his seed.

Shit! Did he seriously just have that thought? What the fuck was wrong with him?

In a fit of anger, he wrapped a broad hand around her delicate throat, but he didn't squeeze. He couldn't. The smartest thing he could do was kill her and just be done with it all. Complications like this were a death sentence for him—and eventually her. Only the logical part of his brain couldn't get the rest of him to agree on jack shit. Even knowing she could change him—that she already had—couldn't make him turn back now. This was a change he was ill prepared for. God, would he survive her? Or would they both burn to ash in an inferno of their own making?

Clear, carob-colored eyes watched him without worry. Generally he struck fear in his fellow man, but not her. Her gaze was calm, waiting for him to make up his mind. Holy hell, this woman was far from the innocent he had thought her to be. Even though he saw she recognized him for the predator he was, she had zero fear of him. Why the fuck not?

"Who the fuck are you?" He'd been wrong before. It did matter who she was and where she'd been.

Azriel had seen humanity in every form there was, but he had never stumbled across an enigma such as she. There really was some innocence there in her face, in her actions, but he knew instinctively she was far from innocent. There was also a purity about her, yet she was sexuality incarnate. On the surface she appeared calm as still water. However, there was a slight catch in her breathing, an excitement she couldn't hide. Her nipples were hard little pebbles pushing against the utilitarian uniform she wore. Yeah, there was a whirlpool under that surface, just waiting to suck him in.

Damned if wasn't going willingly.

"Michelene Brown-Cadeau." The clear but softly spoken response reached out and smacked him dead across his skull.

What the hell had he done?

***

Fuck, fuck, fuck! What the hell had made her admit that? This man, this Azriel lived in the shadow world she'd been born into. That had been obvious at first sight. Actually, she'd known it when she first sensed his presence. Foolishly she'd felt safe enough in her disguise. So why would she go ahead and volunteer information that could very well mean her death? All because, for some unknown reason, she trusted him.

Against all reasoning, she had just placed her life in his hands fully expecting that he would keep her safe. Maybe some part of her was just tired of merely existing. Maybe she was daring fate. No, she knew the truth. For whatever reason, her soul had recognized him from the beginning. This man would never hurt her. He was her salvation.

"There's a bounty on your pretty little head." Her pulse jumped as his finger lazily stroked the column of her neck. His words sunk in, but much like that hand they were no threat to her. He wouldn't be the one to turn her over. For one thing, he didn't need the reward. This was no bounty hunter—he was an assassin, and she was wanted alive.

"I suspect there is." She smiled. Inside she gloated, *You won't be collecting it, will you?*

"Too bad for the people looking for you," he growled. "You're mine now."

Of course she was. She always had been.

CHAPTER 7

Opulence she'd seen before; elegance was nothing new. Michelene wasn't sure which one she'd been expecting on the ride to the top floor. One was often displayed by the nouveau riche to impress, while the other was the result of old money and good breeding. Azriel could've easily been the latter, but she couldn't be sure.

His apartment, however, was neither opulent nor elegant. This may have been one of the most exclusive buildings in the city, and this was certainly the penthouse, but the place itself was Spartan at best. It really didn't look like anyone lived here at all. Minimal in decorations with absolutely no personality, the entire apartment was black, gray and white. It left a person cold.

There was little time to take it all in, however. Azriel marched her through the front rooms, up a carved metal staircase, into a bedroom that took up the entire top floor. No, two-thirds of the top floor. A third was the bathroom, which was their apparent destination. The bathroom should've screamed luxury. A bathtub big enough for at least three adult bodies took up one side of the space, a huge shower with shower jets in the front, the back and at the sides looked bigger than the bathroom in her apartment. Of course there was a water closet, which was also quite spacious. The double sink took up a complete wall. The other was completely made of glass looking over the lights of the city and the Pacific Ocean beyond.

Yeah, it should've been luxurious, if only it had any kind of decoration or personal touches. It looked mostly unused. There was one cup containing a single toothbrush next to one brush on the sink counter. Other than that, it was spotless. Lifeless. If she hadn't been sure before, seeing this apartment confirmed Azriel was exactly what she thought he was. A killer. This was probably one of many places where he crashed whenever he was in town.

"Shit!" The sound of his very real irritation made her jump. Thus far he hadn't shown much emotion. Lust, maybe—even impatience at times. Now he looked at her, looked at the bathtub, then looked back at her. Wow, he looked equal parts frustrated and unsure. That was...surprising.

"Take off your clothes," he groused, obviously displeased about something. And still unsure. What was that about? She was here—she wasn't struggling or complaining.

Not waiting to see whether or not she'd actually do as she'd been told, he stomped over to turn on the shower, then adjusted the water temperature. Okay, wow, so apparently that meant her Eau de Diner cologne really wasn't working for him. Not that she blamed him really—the stench of that place tended to sink in deep despite her best efforts to ward it off. It was just that wetting her hair was problematic seeing as how she didn't have any kind of products to tame her wild natural curls. And she didn't have a stitch to wear after the shower, though she figured she probably wouldn't be wearing anything other than him. Delicious prospect, one that made her tingle in all the right places.

But the hair…

"I won't get your hair wet." Holy crap, he actually smiled when he said that. And not that sardonic asshole grin he had back in the diner. This was gentle, comforting even. It made him look like a real person instead of some deadly, beautiful Terminator robot. "We will get you whatever you need…later. But you're not going back downtown to that rat hole you called yourself living in.

Ever." Fine by her, but she liked where this was going so she decided not to interrupt. "I forbid you to deny yourself any longer. No one will hurt you as long as you're with me, except for me, and I don't plan on letting you go."

Boy, did he ever have no idea what the hell he was declaring there. But his words made her shiver with delicious anticipation. Maybe she should've been scared by that "except for me" bit, but it sounded downright decadent. Maybe she wanted to hurt a little. Maybe she would like it.

No, she would love it.

Still, she was female. Being such, it was just in her nature to test a mate making promises. "So, now you want to hurt me?" Tugging down the front zipper of the god-awful diner uniform, the offensive garment dropped to the floor. Toeing off the sensible service shoes, she shimmied out of the heavy-duty nylons she was forced to wear even in the worst summer heat. Her hands paused at the clasp of her bra, however. Pouting, she shot him her very best puppy-dog look. "I haven't done anything. I'm a good girl."

Where the fuck was all this coming from? Michelene didn't have a clue. It was far from the most daring thing she'd ever done, but teasing a hit man was just not bright. Yet instinct demanded it. And she was rewarded with a look of abject confusion.

But really she was a good girl, more or less. At least she'd pretended to be for the last four years, so she was pretty sure some of it must've rubbed off. Probably not though; she was all too aware there was no such thing as innocence in the world she'd come from. The mud got on you no matter who you were.

Then that look of confusion that had so recently crossed his face was gone. Maybe she shouldn't have teased him. In a blink he was on her, forcing the bra up over her head, fully clasped. The panties were literally ripped off leaving her naked, shivering and so fucking turned on it hurt. Lifting her by the ass, he walked her into the shower. H hadn't bothered to remove his own clothes.

***

Azriel liked to think he was doing just fine holding his shit together, but she had to go and tease him. The matter-of-fact way she disrobed before she got to the bra and panties part had pushed him further than any attempted sensual striptease ever could. But goddamn that "I'm a good girl" bullshit did him in. He had no idea what the hell she was, but a good girl wasn't it. Still, he seriously doubted she understood how bad she could be, how bad he was going to make her be.

The brief flash in her eyes when he first told her to take

off her clothes told him she thought she stunk. The smell of a greasy diner didn't offend him; it was where she worked. What offended him down to his very soul was that she had to work at all. That she had to run and hide. This woman shouldn't ever smell like overused grease and bad food. She should be pampered, perfumed and petted constantly. The shower, which he wished like hell could've been a hot bubble bath, was meant to wash away the last four years of her life. Yes, he was very well aware of how long she'd been missing, but he didn't know why she had chosen to run. No one did. He knew that was four long hard years of bullshit living he wanted to cleanse her of. Wash away the very memory of Gladys and whoever else she'd pretended to be.

A goddamn crime-family princess living in the worst part of the city her family ran was a crime against nature. From what Azriel knew, her father had been a Haitian specializing in running drugs and women from all over the Caribbean, South and Central America and the West Coast of Africa. After his death from mysterious circumstances when Michelene was a child, her mother May Brown, now referred to as Madam Brown, took over the reins, folding them into her own operations of weapons trafficking, prostitution, and porn businesses. Oh, and she sold very young women to the highest bidder.

Azriel had just been starting out when Pierre Cadeau had died, leaving a very lucrative, legitimate job he'd held until the day his parents were cremated. He remembered hearing about the family, about the little girl and boy left behind to a cold bitch of a woman. But Madam Brown grew that business to become a serious player. She was offering a good-sized fortune for her daughter's return. It sucked no one was going to claim that bounty, because Azriel was not about to give her up, the sassy little minx.

With more force than he'd originally intended, he scrubbed her body with his hands. He could've used a washcloth—maybe he should've—but he wanted to feel her skin underneath his hands. Every inch was methodically cleansed with his basic bar of soap. Fuck, but her skin was soft! Only the clothes he still had on were keeping him from taking her right there and then. How was a grown man supposed to hold it together listening to the quiet moans slipping past her lips as his hands worked the muscles of her neck, back, arms and legs? Just that small sign of appreciation had him paying special attention to those areas, kneading until she was lax under his hands. Soon he was going to have to move on to her breasts, and sweet Holy Mother, her ass, and even better, the place he wanted to be worse than a crackhead needed a rock, that pussy.

He was actually trembling a bit as he cupped the generous mounds on her chest. Such generous breasts; they filed his grip to overfilling. Fuck, they felt so good! The caress he was giving her now had nothing to do with cleansing or relieving tension. Now he worked her flesh for pure pleasure.

"I've wanted to touch you like this since I first laid eyes on you," he surprised himself by whispering in her ear. It was something he'd never even admitted to himself until today. Biting softly on her ear, he rolled her nipples between his fingertips. Goddamn, but she was responsive. When she arched her back, her ass pushed back against the erection pushing against his slacks. "Now I get to touch you as often as I want."

And that was going to be very often. Reluctantly he had to let her breasts go, however. There was so much more to get to. Allowing one hand to drift down her soft, gently rounded belly, he pressed between her thighs. The slippery moisture he found inside her pussy had nothing to do with the sprays of water washing over their bodies. Pressing his finger hard against her clit, he used his foot to force her legs open, then pushed his fingers deep inside her cunt.

Damn, she was tight! Barely able to work two fingers inside her, Azriel started to pant. She was going to choke the shit out of his dick. That wasn't going to stop him. He had to have to her. He needed to take her with a drive he couldn't begin to put into words.

"Come for me, baby," he demanded. "Show me what a good girl you really are."

With broken cry, that's exactly what she did. Her body tensed, her pussy spasming wildly against his finger. Fuck, that was sweet! He couldn't wait to make her do that again. And again. Ass many fucking times as he could manage before they both collapsed into a mindless heap.

CHAPTER 8

As soon as the last tremors quieted, Michelene whirled, yanking at Azriel's soaking shirt. Fuck her hair—that was a worry for tomorrow. All that mattered right now was having nothing between them. Her own ferocity should've scared her, but honestly she couldn't really focus clearly on anything other than this wild, animalistic drive to take and be taken. It was new, this kind of attraction. It was undefinable, but shit, it was consuming her.

All she could think about was the way she hungered to taste his wet skin, how much she wanted to feel him against her, without those damn clothes in her way! Ripping the shirt open, it didn't matter to her she couldn't quite get the thing off his massive shoulders. She needed to bite him—so she did, sucking on the little half-moon shapes her teeth left in his flesh. And he let her, over and over again; he stood there letting her ravage his smooth chest. Her finger curled into the light sprinkling of chest hairs, yanking them hard on purpose. Fuck, what was this he was doing to her? She felt feral, like she wanted to make him feel her.

When her teeth sank into the dusky points of his nipples, a strong grasp snatched her head back. The grip on her hair was painful, but yessss that pain felt divine. The way he looked down at her, those ghostly silver eyes burned her to her marrow. Ravenous, that's how he looked. Like he was either going to eat her alive or choke her out. How in the hell was that sexy? But when his eyes drifted to her throat, up to her lips, then clashed with her eyes she could've melted into a puddle right there in the shower. God, his body was taut. It screamed out he was going to explode. She wanted to see that. Hell, she wanted to experience it.

Reaching out defiantly, she unbuckled his belt slowly, licking her lips, deliberately exaggerating the movement. A fierce frown pierced his brow though he made no move to stop her. So she unbuttoned the top of his pants, unzipping them before she dropped to her knees, taking his pants with her. Funny how even though she was kneeling, he'd never let go of her hair. Michelene didn't care. She liked it. Laying her cheek against his thigh, she had to force his feet up to take his pants off completely.

Had he not wanted the damn things off, there would've been no way she could've lifted his feet. But he made her work for it. That irked her more than a little. How dare he have such control when she had clearly lost all of hers? So she ran the sharp points of her teeth against the skin of his thighs, leisurely working her way up until she got to his pelvis. So far she'd avoided the angry-looking cock that stood so proud, bobbing ever so slightly in front of her face. It was beautiful. So full, so long and thick. He hadn't worn underwear, so there was nothing between them. And that dick called to her. Some primal demand that had her tongue sticking out to circle the reddish-purple head.

The hiss that burst from his lips was worth it, but the grip on her hair once more pulled her back.

"Have you done this before?"

His words confused the hell out of her. Done what exactly? And he looked genuinely concerned, which was just weird. Most men she knew would've just forced her head down on them, not pulled her back. And how the hell did he know she wasn't as experienced as she was pretending to be? At least not experienced with the voluntary attraction. His eyes held knowledge he shouldn't have, and she didn't want that right now. Couldn't deal with it.

"Yes, I have." No way she'd volunteer more than that.

"Shit."

Just like that, she found herself being hauled out of the shower and placed on the counter far more gently than she'd ever expected. The hands pulling her thighs apart were neither forceful nor gentle. They were insistent.

"Keep your feet on the edge of the counter," Azriel ordered, but he was no longer looking at her face. All his focus was centered on her exposed pussy. "Don't. Move."

Right. Don't move. That should be about as easy as restoring her virginity.

A thick finger ran along her puffy outer lips. Just a feather of a touch, over and over again. The bathroom might have been massive, but it was starting to feel stuffy, crowded even. God, he wasn't doing much more than teasing her but she felt surrounded by him. The sound of her own panting was almost obscene. And he'd said don't move. If he didn't stop playing with her she was going to jump him!

"Such a pretty pussy on such a pretty little girl." Opening her labia as he spoke, he started to flick at her clit. Damn, his words were so wrong, so very naughty. But she was a long way from being a little girl. She should've hated those words. Should've wanted to slap them out of his mouth, but they laid her bare more than her nakedness could. "This is my pretty pussy now. You understand that, don't you?" To punctuate his statement, his fingers ground down on her clit. Hard. Fuck if it didn't feel like heaven.

A cry escaped her lips as her body jerked upward in immediate response.

SMACK!

The flat of his palm slammed across her pussy; the wetness from the shower mixed with her own overflowing natural juices made the sting burn with white-hot heat. Fuck, fuck, fuck, but that hurt so damn good! It was like the heat melted into her skin then began to caress her from the inside. She hadn't even noticed his fingers had skillfully entered her, thrusting fast and hard as she could only sit there and whimper.

"Look at me, Michelene." The dark purr was almost enough to make her come. Shit, she really needed to come. "Let me see you. Watch me watching you, baby."

Oh, had she closed her eyes? She hadn't noticed. That statement, though—could a man possibly say anything any hotter? It was just so—

SMACK!

"Open your fucking eyes!"

Well, shit, who knew they had closed again? She didn't remember doing that. But she did know she wanted badly to hurt him back. Not because she was mad about the smack to her cunt; that was simply delicious. She wanted to bite him, scratch him, dig her nails into his skin just because this total stranger had gotten down deep inside her very core and looked at all her darkest secrets without asking, without saying a word. And she couldn't hate him for it though she really, really wanted to. He was forcing vulnerability, giving her exactly what she needed. What she would've never in a million years admitted she needed.

"There you are." He smirked while curving his fingers upwards to find that spongy bundle of nerves deep inside her with deadly precision. That's a good girl. Now come."

***

Of course he hadn't expected her to stay completely still. He would've been damned pissed if she had. Fuck, but she reacted perfectly to everything he did. His cock was drizzling pre-cum all over the fucking place, he wanted in her so damn bad! As soon as her back arched—as he was beginning to notice was one of her telltale signs of an impending orgasm—his mouth descended, latching on to a bountiful breast and sucking fervently on the nipple. Her cunt flooded, tightening painfully hard down on his fingers. Man, his dick was in serious trouble.

That was one seriously tight-ass pussy. He wasn't a small man. For the first time ever, he was honestly worried. God knows he didn't really want to hurt her, not like that. Something told him she'd been hurt like that already. He needed to show her passion, no matter how ferocious, was nothing to fear. So yes, he would smack that hungry wet cunt, bite her nipple, smack that lush ass, but didn't want to cause her real physical harm.

Waiting until her trembles calmed somewhat, Azriel knelt between her spread thighs. She really did have a pretty pussy, all groomed and perfect. With the schedule he'd witnessed, when had she found the time? But he was grateful she had. It was adorable. Leaning forward, he inhaled her natural scent. The unique smell of her arousal was like a fucking drug. He had to wrap a fist around his cock just to give the poor thing some kind of relief.

Using the flat of his tongue, he licked from clit to taint then flicked that wicked tongue from side to side all the way back up, concentrating on her clit. After tormenting the deep-pink nubbin of nerves, he closed his lips around it, sucking ever so softly. Michelene tried to jerk against him, but he held her in place with one hand. She was a curvy woman, so fucking soft and perfect for a long, hard ride. Yet he had no problem keeping her right where he wanted her. Azriel wasn't about to be denied the meal he'd missed out on earlier. This was the one he'd wanted all along anyway. He wanted her screams, her broken sobs of pleasure so intense they couldn't be put into words. Damn it, he wanted more than that. He wanted her to forget everything and everyone that came before him. He needed her to fall completely apart so he could pick up the pieces and put her back together again.

Working his fingers back inside her compact channel was easier this time, thank God. Gradually increasing the suction on her clit, he moved slowly but forcefully, spreading his fingers inside her as much as he could. He was going to need room in there. Every a few seconds, he would switch directions and stroke her g-spot just enough to make her yank on his hair, but not enough to let her come. He didn't let her find release until his hand was coated with her sweet honey. Then he sucked hard, pistoning his fingers inside relentlessly.

Fuck, watching her come was a gorgeous sight. Hell the woman was nothing less than beauty personified. He wanted to keep watching her come, but he needed to be inside her in the worst fucking way.

"Get up and turn around." Only once again, he couldn't wait for her to do it. So he lifted her off the counter, set her on her feet then turned her around. It took less than a second, and it was still too long.

He'd wanted to take her for the first time on his bed. Actually, he had thought about tying her to his bed, but he was all out of patience. Nothing in the universe mattered more than getting inside her right fucking now.

"Keep your eyes open," he ordered, staring her down in the mirror as he sawed the head of his cock into the slick opening of her pussy. "Don't close them. Don't look away from me."

To reinforce his command, he grabbed hold to the back of her neck, cursing himself for not thinking to take her hair out of that damn bun.

Later. Later he would explore her more thoroughly. Right now—fuck, he just needed to be inside her. Needed it more than he needed his trigger finger.

Fuuuuuuuuuuuck, he was in trouble.

CHAPTER 9

Oh God, she so hadn't been ready. Even though he was so careful, working that impossibly thick cock inside her gradually, when she felt all of him, every inch buried deep inside her, she panicked. It was too much! She was just too full. But sweet holy fuck, that burning pain felt glorious.

"Open. Your. Fucking. Eyes." Azriel was practically snarling, his breathing not much more than heavy pants.

Michelene's eyes snapped open on command only to be snared by the piercing glare of silver orbs watching her in the mirror. Every inch the predator now, he looked as if he were about to devour her. He looked…dangerous. Vicious. So damn sexy it hurt. Her stomach did little flips at the way he was looking at her. There was the same ravenous hunger she felt reflected clearly n his heated gaze.

Raw, unabashed lust just for her. But there was nothing wrong or off about this kind of lust. It was pure; it was right. The burn in his eyes just intensified the burn in her cunt, setting off a much deeper yearning, one she was unfamiliar with and didn't quite understand. It caused her pussy to flood even more, the wetness somehow seeping past the dick that gave her no room for anything but him, coating her thighs. She'd be embarrassed if she'd been able to focus on anything other than the man who kept her gaze locked in his.

"You're so fucking beautiful."

Sweet baby Jesus, why did he have to say it like that? Like a prayer or something. And she could say nothing in return. Not when he was starting to move. Slow, measured strokes that brought his cock all the way out to the very tip before slamming back inside her grasping channel. Harder, faster. There was no looking away, not enough air to scream; the most she could do was lean forward, bracing herself on her forearms. There was nothing left to do but feel him. Every inch, every vein, every throb of his cock she felt against the ultrasensitive walls of her channel.

Something momentous was building inside her. She felt it starting at her very core. Starting like the soft fluttering of butterfly wings, it built and built in intensity. With every powerful thrust the feeling got stronger. This wasn't the gentle, rolling orgasm she was used to. This was violent, a turbulent force of fucking nature, and there was nothing she could do to stop it if she wanted to. And she didn't want to.

"You're going to come for me, aren't you, baby?" Jesus, the man even sounded like obscene sex personified. "I can feel you spasming all around me." Without breaking contact, he leaned over her back and bit the area where her shoulder and neck met. "You're squeezing me. Making me want to flood that sweet little pussy with my cum."

Oh God, oh God—that should not sound so hot. It was base. It was magnificent. Heaven help her, there was nothing she could do to hold back the tidal wave that crashed over her. There was no soft beginning that built gradually. Her orgasm slammed into her every bit as much as his hips did, robbing her of air, sight, or coherent thought. What was this? People just didn't have sex like this, did they? And him, damn his devilish soul, hadn't missed a motherfucking stroke.

"Ummm, that's it, baby," he moaned into her ear. "Come for me again, and I'll come for you."

Again? But that couldn't be—

"Oh, fuck, Azriel!" Her knees locked, her body freezing for a few moments before beginning to shake.

Where the hell had that come from? Damn it, she

couldn't stop the convulsions coming from deep inside her womb, radiating outward. One iron-strong arm banded around her, anchoring her to earth when she would've fallen flat on her face.

"That was beautiful, sweetheart," he purred. Damned if she didn't preen just a little. "Feel me, feel what you're making me do."

God, yes! The throbbing in his cock drove her wild as he shot load after load of hot sperm inside her. The feeling alone set off yet another chain of explosions in her pussy, and the finger pressed against her clit didn't do a damn thing to help her calm down.

"I can't," she gasped, afraid she wouldn't be able to take much more.

"You can, and you will," came the immediate definitive response.

Then he took the finger on her clit and started rubbing in little circles, using her own juices as lubricant. Fast. Relentless. Why the hell was he still hard? "Come again. Now."

Obeying his command, Michelene flew apart. Again. Then passed out.

CHAPTER 10

Sleep wasn't going to happen tonight, so Azriel didn't even bother trying. Everything about his own behavior puzzled him. Twice more he'd taken Michelene until she was sobbing. Then he fed her, and then fucked her again. As she slept peacefully in his bed, he had to get up. That woke her up, he guessed, though she made no move to let him know. So he said nothing. And he didn't go back to the bed. There was no lying next to the woman and not wanting to fuck her. So he sat in a chair across the room watching her watch him. There was no way she wasn't exhausted, yet she wasn't any closer to sleep than he was.

Maybe despite finding obvious pleasure in his arms, she was afraid of him. That would be wise. He was not an easy man. Hell, he was barely a man at all. He was a machine of death. That was what he lived for; it was all he did. But he seriously doubted that bothered her at all. And she did know who he was. He'd seen the recognition in her eyes. And why wouldn't she? The life she lived before her barren existence downtown would've have given her knowledge far beyond that of the average person. There were so many questions about Michelene Brown-Cadeau, but it galled the shit out of him to have to ask them. People volunteered information to him—not that it would stop him from killing them. By the time he was hired, it was too late for the mark. But her? His Michelene gave him nothing.

Damn it, he was going to have to ask.

"I've heard of your family," he finally said, really unsure how one went about interrogating their lover.

"Most people in your line of work have." Smooth reply. Still gave him jack shit by way of answers to the puzzle of how she ended up hiding from her family.

"I like killing." That wasn't going for the shock factor so much as it was the absolute truth. He'd just never said the words out loud before.

"You can just ask me what you want to know," she replied, rolling onto her back. The wall of windows let in more than enough light to make out that body sprawled on his bed. So fucking gorgeous. Hills and valleys, plump in all the right places; she was a fucking goddess. His cock started to jump. He'd just fucked her no less than four times and he still wanted her.

"Your father was Pierre Cadeau from Haiti—ran women and drugs until his death. Then your mother May Brown took over and combined it with her family business, adding slave trading to the mix just because she's a sadistic bitch like that." Azriel knew calling her mother a sadistic bitch was a bit much perhaps, but that was exactly what the woman was. "Your mother never remarried but has had a string of lovers, usually her bodyguards. You have a brother, Pierre Jr., who is a year and a half older than you. He can't stand your mother but is her second in command anyway. Did I about cover it?"

He didn't mention how he knew because it didn't really matter. He'd expected her to be…something. Shocked? Impressed? Maybe both. Just not neither.

"My brother goes by Pierre," she stated calmly. "Don't ever call him Junior."

That was it.

Maybe she thought he would be intimidated by her family. The very idea that he would be intimidated by anyone at all was offensive, but they had just officially met. Funny how it kind of felt like they had been dating forever, but just finally had the chance now to consummate their relationship.

With a heavy sigh she sat up. To her credit, she didn't try to cover her nakedness with a sheet like he hadn't just screwed her silly.

"I know my brother is probably looking for me, as well as a few other people." She spoke softly, as though she felt bad about something. "I think he has to punish me for what I did. He doesn't really have a choice. Not to exact retribution would make him look weak. I just don't think he has looked very hard for me. I would like to think a part of him doesn't want to ever find me."

Punished? Retribution? He hadn't heard anything like that. Only that the spoiled daughter of Madam Brown ran away from an arranged marriage. Things like that were big in the underworld. Why did she believe only her brother was looking for her and not her mother? Moreover, why the hell would she voluntarily hide in the slums? If her brother and her mother were at odds, couldn't she have just gone to him to get out of a marriage she didn't want? Azriel was damn glad she had run away, but nothing about Michelene made rational sense.

"Yes," he answered carefully. "Your brother is looking for you. As is your mother. But I guess for different reasons. I can understand that." Only he really didn't. Rumors were always rife among the criminal classes, so he had never paid close attention. Before today the missing daughter of a flesh peddler meant nothing to him. "Whatever the reasons are…"

There was something about her that wasn't quite right. One second she was fine, the next she was staring at him, eyes wide, her mouth slightly open, looking very much afraid. No, she was terrified. He didn't think she was even breathing. What the fuck?

In seconds he was by her side, the instinct to protect so strong he wanted to kill someone. He just had no idea who he should kill.

"No one will touch you." Not ever. Even after death he would protect his woman with the sheer force of his motherfucking will. "Tell me what scares you and I will eliminate it, no matter what it is." What the hell had he said to scare the shit out her? He couldn't recall anything she didn't know already.

Plucking her up, he sat her on his lap, cradling her in his arms like a baby. How natural it felt to hold her like this. Generally, Azriel couldn't stand any touch that wasn't necessary to achieve a goal. Getting close to a mark, sex, or his parents were the only time he could recall experiencing a voluntary touch. It wasn't something he encouraged. But this—this just felt right. Great, now he was getting redundant in his own damn head.

"I thought I killed her." It was nothing more than a

broken whisper. Just a wisp of air carrying the faintest amount of sound. "I meant to kill her. God, I wanted her dead so bad. I slit her throat and ran. I didn't stop; I just took off. There was so much blood I thought she had to be dead. How could she still be alive?"

Azriel said nothing. Confessions—any kind, really—couldn't be coerced no matter what the movies and popular fiction led one to believe. If you tortured some helpless sap, they blurted out whatever the hell they thought you wanted to hear. If you tried to coax it out of someone with sweet talk and bullshit, you would get a load of bullshit in return. This wasn't war; they weren't dealing with soldiers. Criminals lied; the families of criminals lied even better. Truth was often subjective in this life they led. True confessions? They came from the gut, an overwhelming need to purge, and there was no way of guessing the trigger. It could be apple pie for some.

What Azriel needed from Michelene now was a true confession, because he needed to know what he was dealing with. There would be no letting her go, not even back into the bosom of her family. He didn't fucking share—he could give a shit if they were talking about her mother or brother—she belonged to him now. Her family had quite obviously failed in protecting her, otherwise she wouldn't be here now. Whatever scared her would be dealt with. Then she could call her family members or some shit. Maybe once a month visitation. Supervised.

In any event, he just held her, silently willing her to keep talking. Eventually she did.

"She was never much of a mother, I guess." Thank the fucking cosmos her voice had gotten stronger. The pain that had been there before, the hopelessness ripped at his gut. He didn't want to tolerate her pain; he wanted it dead. "Most of the time she left Pierre and me with whoever was available. When my father was alive it was always him, even though she knew what he was like. Who he was." Son of a bitch. Sucker punched didn't even begin to explain how he felt. It was too bad the son of a bitch was dead. But he could still kill her mother. "Then my father was dead, and we got a real nanny of sorts. And I grew up. My mother noticed. There are a lot of men she dealt with who—"

"Stop." Fuck, he couldn't take it. He'd thought he could, but shit. It wasn't anything he hadn't heard before, but he'd never heard it from her. The pain all bottled up inside this woman was killing him. He needed to brace himself, then help her deal with it. But fuck, he had to deal with it his damn self. "She's dead." And he would kill that bitch unfit to be called a mother. It was as good as done.

Just because he didn't understand maternal love didn't

mean he didn't know what it was supposed to look like. It was not like this.

"No, she is mine. I will finish what I started." Okay, that shocked him. It was the last thing he'd expected her to say. "Only I won't fail this time."

"No, baby, you won't," he promised holding her tighter. Because he would be right there by her side to make damn sure that bitch was dead.

***

They weren't here. It had taken him all day to find which damn beach house belonged to Seth. Then he'd had to find the perfect hiding spot in a place far too exposed for his tastes. He should've brought along a weapon—a gun, knife, something. But that hardly mattered because they weren't fucking here! Where had that animal taken his angel? What the hell was he doing to her right now? He had to find her! She was his! His only hope.

Head throbbing, he had to slow the rising tide of his rage. When his anger got the best of him he couldn't think clearly. This was not over. Sooner or later, Seth would be found. He would turn over every rock until he discovered where the filthy bastard had taken Michelene. She was his! She was the promise of a normal life.

Resources. He had resources, and it was high time he used them. His family sneered at him because of the way he was. All he had to do was explain that part of his life was behind him now. All he needed to be well was Michelene. Yes, his family would surely help if it meant he would no longer be an embarrassment. And he knew exactly who to call.

CHAPTER 11

"What exactly did you tell that fucked-up little freak who was here last week?"

Munoz wasn't the smartest of the young and dumb to grace Pierre's mother's bed, but the man was ambitious. That ambition had become his downfall. Pierre had always made a habit of disposing of ambitious men who graced his mother's bed. They tended to get delusions of grandeur. The Brown-Cadeau family was his. And so he would get rid of the filth his mother had brought into the family business and get back to good old crime. It would be so much easier to buy into the legitimate world of power. No more slave trafficking, no underage hookers—hell, no hookers at all. And no more fucking drugs. All these motherfuckers who came from narco states were disgusting to him. There was no loyalty, no honor. Yeah,

Pierre wasn't a choirboy. But he had fucking ethics.

But Munoz—this little bitch boy had crossed the line. Selling out his sister to a psycho? Oh, hell, no, this bitch was going to pay.

"I didn't tell—" Before the lying could even start, Pierre punched him low in the gut, the grabbed him around the throat. He didn't squeeze too hard, just enough to hurt.

Like most of his mother's lovers, Munoz had listened to the bullshit his mother spouted about him. They never suspected that underneath the charm and fancy suit, Pierre didn't give a shit about much. He'd rather kill a man than listen to his crap. They thought him soft, thought he was afraid to get his hands dirty. Nothing could be further from the truth; he just knew how to pick his battles. He watched, waited, listened. Sooner or later a fool would show his hand. And if the opponent wasn't a fool, well, then he would know how to proceed.

This man was a fool. Worse, he was a threat to Pierre's only real family. His sister.

"I'm not in the mood to play." Pierre tsked softly. "Do you really want to test me? Do you think May will miss you? Have you ever wondered what happened to the ones that came before you? You think you're better? Smarter? You damn sure aren't prettier."

The fucker really did believe himself to be smarter. Maybe even prettier. Pierre could see it in the flash of anger in Munoz's eyes. Oh, but the bastard was going to pay for that. Pierre had planned on giving him a quick death. That plan flew straight out the window. Motherfuckers were really going to have to learn not to piss him off.

Releasing Munoz, Pierre signaled for the men waiting quietly behind the idiot. Men Munoz had believed to be his friends. Men who had always been loyal to Pierre.

"This must be your lucky day." Pierre smiled. It was far from his lucky day. It was going to be the worst. Finally Munoz understood what kind of shit creek he had managed to float up. The man started to sweat profusely, his eyes darting around the room looking for any kind of help. Help that was nowhere to be seen. "I've decided to allow you to continue breathing…for now.

It was a lie. Pierre was going to kill him. But he was going to make him bleed first.

Giving Munoz his back, he retrieved his machete from a nearby table. The blade gleamed wickedly as it caught the sunlight. Pierre always kept his favorite weapon close at hand. Watching out of the corner of his eye, he saw Munoz begin to shake as Pierre picked up the machete, saw him shake harder when Pierre nicked his own finger so that a single fat drop of blood welled up on the fingertip. Yeah, the blade was hella sharp. Pierre babied it, polishing and sharpening constantly.

Eyes bulging, Munoz began to sputter out everything, as Pierre had known he would. For one thing, Munoz had no idea why Pierre was really pissed off enough to end him.

"I told him where Azriel Seth's beach house was!" Munoz cried. "And I told him to make sure to take Michelene somewhere far away so she could never return." And that was the mistake. But Pierre said nothing, allowing him to continue. "Isn't that what you want?" No, that was far from what he wanted, still Pierre said nothing. "Your mother wants her to follow in her footsteps! She wants to give the business over to her just because she managed to hook up with Seth."

That's because their mother was no fool. Azriel Seth was an independent contractor. The best in the business. If he had gotten with Michelene for more than a night, the rumors alone would be a coup for the family.

As tempting as it was to separate the man's head from his body, Pierre managed to stay his hand. Barely. He already knew what Munoz had told the sniveling little worm who'd somehow managed to find his sister when no one else had been able to. That wasn't the information he was after. But damn, it was infuriating to hear out of this snake's mouth what everyone assumed. Pierre didn't hate his sister, no matter their mother's plans. Quite the opposite. There was no one he loved more in the world, but he felt an enormous amount of guilt for never being there when she really needed him. Now he just wanted to make sure she was safe. If it were true Seth had taken a liking to her, then she was in the safest hands she could possibly be in. But he needed to let her know he was here for her now. He would be here for her until the end of time. He only wished she'd succeeded in killing their mother.

"And how would you know the location of Azriel Seth's beach house?" Pierre asked mildly, though the tip of his machete ran across Munoz's cheeks. Blood appeared immediately, dripping down his face in a parody of the very real tears that also ran down the man's face. God, he wanted to kill him. But that was secondary to the main objective. He needed only to find his sister before his mother or the crow man that had come sniffing around.

When Munoz failed to speak to his satisfaction, babbling about how loyal he was to the family, Pierre really did lose patience.

"Put him on his knees," he told the men holding Munoz. As soon as they did, he ran the blade over

Munoz's shirt. The material fell to the sides without so much of a whisper. Then he ran the blade in an X pattern across the chest. Deeper than the cuts on his cheeks, but not enough to inflict serious damage. "I am not a patient man." Another cut across the abdomen made him scream. "And I do so enjoy carving…things. It calms me."

"M-my cousin! Rico—Rico Cruz!" Munoz screeched out. He began to babble as much as he bled. "Rico was pissed because Seth refused a contract—"

"So?" Pierre was puzzled enough to stop and listen. Seth was known for turning down contracts, mostly without explanation. It was all part of the man's mystique. The other part of his legend was that he never failed to make a hit. Ever.

"The contract was on someone…someone in this family. But I don't know who I swear. I am just supposed to give my cousin information." That was a lie. Why did they always try to lie near the end? It never saved their worthless lives. "Rico, he is really mad about not getting your sister…"

"Not getting my who?" No. There was no way Pierre had heard that right.

"Michelene. Your mother, she sold her to Rico—"

The words were cut off as Pierre cleaved Munoz's head from his neck. Really he hadn't meant to so soon. He had wanted to play with the man for a while. But his words were...

His mother had tried to sell Michelene? Before now he'd had no idea why his sister had tried to slice May's neck open. Now that he knew, he wanted to kill the bitch himself. But this death wasn't his to give. One thing was for damn sure, after all the things his little sister had gone through in her life, she deserved ultimate retribution. And Pierre would move heaven and earth to make sure she got it. Madam May Brown was a dead woman; she just didn't know it yet.

***

Two weeks! That filthy animal'd had his precious Michelene for two whole weeks! Why hadn't Seth brought her back to the beach house? No one knew where any of his other places were. Rico had sworn to him this was the place Seth was most likely to be found when he wasn't on a job. Where the hell could he be?

Head pounding mercilessly, he paced the hot, dry sand, trying to put his thoughts in coherent order. How could he find her? God, what was that vile man doing to his angel? Surely by now Seth had touched her, caressed her soft skin, seen her without clothes, kissed those full supple lips—

No, no, no, no! He couldn't allow himself to think

about those things. It didn't matter anyway. He'd cleanse her, just like he used to. Purge her of the evil inside so she could be pure again, those sparkling brown eyes shining with unshed tears as she felt the forgiveness he had given her, felt the love. Then, then she could be his. His long-dormant cock stirred remembering how she'd looked at him, how she looked as she trudged to and from work, living a life of repentance. Her soul was pure; it always had been.

The apartment! He would start there. Sooner or later she would come back for her things, especially the box under her bed where she treasured his gifts. She loved him, only him. She knew only he could offer her a life lived in the light. Besides, once he was there he could scour the city for any trace the hit man had left. There were always traces. Men were never as clever as they thought themselves to be. He was superior. He had intellect where Seth only had weapons.

They hadn't left the state; he knew that because Rico was monitoring that. All he needed to do was stay calm, and he could find them—he could find her. Then everything would be okay. She could save him, and he would save her.

CHAPTER 12

"I'm going to need clothes." Honestly, Michelene wasn't overly concerned about clothing. The last two weeks wearing nothing more than one of Azriel's shirts had been just fine with her. Made the deliverymen, who brought food and bath and beauty products, do a double take a time or two. Frankly she loved seeing the possessive side of Azriel. A couple of times he actually growled at the delivery guys if their gazes rest on her a little too long. But she was starting to feel a little restless. Being confined to a home was something she had been used to four years ago, but the last few years of relative freedom had been nice.

"Perhaps," came the noncommittal answer.

He liked her nude. Oddly she was okay with that. There'd never been an occasion in her life she'd voluntarily gone without clothing aside from showering or changing.

Never had she lingered in a bubble bath as she did now, or just stroll around without a stitch one. It had never been safe. It was shocking to her how easy it was to be completely bare in front of this man. In fact, she loved the way his eyes followed her when she was nude, the way he touched her. There were times he could be so very gentle. Yet she really didn't think he knew how to be anything other than completely dominating in bed.

Michelene found herself confessing all kinds of things from her childhood. Things she never told anyone. Some parts of her life upset him visibly, though he hadn't told her to stop since that first night, so she never told him the worst of it. She didn't really want to talk about those things anyway. It was weird, because he had to have seen worse. Yet that tic would show in his jawline when she spoke of her mother and some of the things Madam May had forced her to do.

When she spoke of her mother, not only did the tic bulge out of his jaw; it would begin to pulsate. His eyes would narrow into slits, burning not with hatred, or even anger, but straight death. If she were on the outside looking in, maybe she'd be terrified when he looked like that. As it was, she found it sexy. There was nothing about Azriel Michelene found frightening. It was thrilling to see him so upset on her behalf. Here was a man who wouldn't hesitate not only to kill for her, but help her kill anyone she felt needed killing. Quite simply the perfect man for her.

Michelene also knew this unexplained thing between them mystified him at times. Some nights he sat silently in the corner, watching her with a frown marring that majestic brow. Other times when they were talking, he would tell her tidbits about his life before contract killing, things about his childhood or his parents. He seemed surprised when he caught himself doing that. And pissed at himself. He would withdraw for a little while after that, or fuck her. Hard. It made her smile because she knew what he had yet to come to terms with, and that was okay.

He showed her in so many ways the things he didn't say. Right now, Azriel seemed fascinated with the feel of her skin underneath his fingertips. Lying on her stomach, she sighed as he ran his fingers up and down her spine, every now and then stopping to kiss one spot or another. How normal it felt; like they were any other couple just lying around on a lazy afternoon. As loath as she was to break the spell, there were cold hard facts they needed to deal with.

"You do remember people are looking for me, right?" God, she really didn't want their idyllic existence to end, but staying here was bound to catch the attention of someone.

"There have been people looking for you for the last four years," he replied glibly, shifting so his heavy leg lay across hers. "They either aren't very interested in finding you or they suck at finding people."

Well, that all depended on who was in charge of doing the searching. If it were Pierre, then no, he might not be all that interested in finding her. His efforts might be halfhearted at best, especially if her mother wanted to make an example out of her. Michelene hadn't stayed hidden for so long because she was afraid of her brother. It was May's underlings that had scared her shitless. Power hungry, ruthless, they wouldn't hesitate to make an example out of her. May loved to dangle the possibility of helping her rule in front of her lovers. Had Michelene really killed her they would be chomping at the bit to try to wrestle the reins from Pierre; the perfect way to do that would be to extract vengeance for May's death. But seeing as how Michelene hadn't killed her mother, what she could expect was much worse. It was a damn good thing she had chosen to stay in the same city as her family, living in decrepit conditions. She was considered spoiled, never having done a hard day's work in her life. Living a life of drudgery would be the last thing they expected.

One thing about May Brown was she never forgave a

slight, and knifing her neck was definitely that. Someone was bound to talk. A delivery man, apartment maintenance staff. These were people you just couldn't control. And the incident at the diner had probably been talked about for days. Inevitably someone would hear something, then questions would be asked. Azriel hadn't been the least bit incognito. He'd been the opposite.

"They didn't find me because before I actually laid eyes on you, I'd never stood out." With an aggravated grunt, she flipped over, scooting away from his distracting touch. "I can't stay here. Since you got rid of the only clothes I had, at least give me a lift back to my apartment."

Like a child deprived of his favorite toy, Azriel actually pouted. It was funny as hell. She was willing to bet anything he thought he was scowling, but that was a pout on his face. Lip sticking out and everything.

"This is your apartment," he stated mulishly, once again deliberately missing the point.

"My apartment is on the other side of town. It's where all my stuff is. Like clothes. So I can find a new place to hide."

"If you are referring to the hovel where you used to reside, all of the things there have been gathered up and disposed of. There was nothing personal there anyway, and I seriously doubted you wanted that sad collection of so-called gifts from the man who thought he could stalk you."

Wow. He spoke as if it were all so simple, so reasonable. In a really twisted way, it made perfect sense because she really didn't have a damn thing personal there. All that she'd had that meant anything to her, she'd left behind when she ran. Then again, they were twisted. For two people who lived lives so far outside the norm, this weird dynamic they had wasn't all that shocking. Azriel was a heavy-handed kind of guy. She really should've expected something like this.

Still, just accepting what he'd had done would make her appear weak. It made no difference she wasn't really upset, nor was she scared. Really, what he'd done was smart. All the people downtown knew about her were fake names and that dingy apartment. But a stand must be made on general principles. It would do him good to confuse him a little.

"You had no right to do that!" she exploded in a fair facsimile of anger. To make it look really good, she jumped from the bed to her feet, placing her hands on her hips. "Those were my things! They were all I had." Okay, that might be pouring it on a bit thick. She had three trust funds.

"You had no personal items, and the clothes were cheap." Oh, the genuine bafflement all over his face was priceless.

It was hard to keep up the facade with him looking all gloriously sexy, all male, all clueless. What was really funny was the way he was starting to get hard in the face of her pretend anger. It was impossible not to grow wet in response.

"It doesn't matter if they were cheap!" she retorted, stomping her feet for effect. "They were mine! Has it ever occurred to you I might not want to walk around naked for however long it amuses you? Maybe I'd like to go out, or go to the theatre, see a play or something!"

That was pouring it on way too thick. She could care less about any of those things, though a walk in the fresh air would be nice.

It hadn't occurred to him though; she could see that all over his face. He looked well and truly chastened. And pissed. How delicious. Holding her breath, she had to bite the inside of her cheek to keep from smiling as he rose, just as nude as she was, to tower over her. God, the controlled menace in that tall, muscular body was intoxicating. She craved that power. Craved his darkness.

"However long it amuses me?" The low rumble of his voice was like the thunder warning of the coming storm. Yes, she wanted that storm.

"You are mine, now and forever—mine. I will provide

for you. You want clothes—I will buy them. When I choose to. I prefer you naked, so you will be naked." That hot gaze swept her, licking fire all across her skin. "No one would dare to harm you. Yes, there are people looking for you, but you are never, ever unprotected. We will leave when it's time to do so. Not before. And Michelene, I keep what is mine. No one dares take what belongs to me. Do you understand?"

Nothing could keep the smile off her face now. That was exactly what she wanted to hear. "Yes. Thank you."

CHAPTER 13

The woman was deliberately provoking him, and this was far from the first time. Knowing that didn't stop his blood from boiling that she would actually insinuate he would get tired of her. Or that he would allow any harm to come to her. Seriously? Like he could ever get tired of her. The woman could be four different people in one day. She was funny, sexy, passionate, caring and yet in a weird way innocent without being annoying. And she was his. All that she was belonged to him.

Looking down at that upturned face, those soulful eyes flashing outrage he knew damn well she didn't feel, he felt a fresh wave of anger wash over him. MINE! That single word encompassed so much, but not nearly enough. No one could take her, no one could fucking touch her. He would completely lose his shit. They may not have known each other long, but that didn't make a damn bit of difference. No one else in this world could make him feel—hell, just make him feel. Anger, lust, pity, an aching need that just wouldn't go away. And this strange, undefinable warmth that radiated from deep in his gut just touching her, watching her, or...

Fuck, he had to be inside her like now.

Reaching down, he clasped her ass cheeks and lifted, heaving her onto the bed. Damn her, she actually smiled at him, like this was what she was after all along. Maybe it was. He could never be entirely certain when it came to her. He did know she wanted him. In the few seconds it took for him to drop her on the bed, then fall on top of her, her legs were open, thighs wide to accommodate him. Later there would be foreplay. He would drive her out of her mind teasing, driving her close to the edge then backing off, playing with her soft, yielding body until she begged for him. But right now, the driving need to be a part of her—there was no way he could resist.

Pinning her hands above her head, he plunged inside her in one powerful thrust. Sweet holy fuck, how could a pussy be so tight, yet so wet? It was almost like her body was taunting him every bit as much as her words were. It wouldn't make a difference; he was too far gone to be anything but completely entranced. Nothing mattered but this—driving his cock balls-deep inside her over and over again until they were both too exhausted to move.

"Look at me," he growled. "Keep your fucking eyes on me." There was something about the way she looked when they came together like this. It made him feel like a fucking god.

"Yes, Daddy."

Shit.

His cock jumped inside her, little goddamn tease. There was something about the way she said that; it called to some long dormant part in him. He never thought he would be that guy, the one who got off on hearing his woman talk to him like that, but damned if it didn't drive him crazy. Maybe it was sick on some level, but who had time to give a shit about conventions? When she called him that it made him want to protect her, care for her, fuck her until he couldn't see straight.

His hips increased speed and force. It wasn't planned. He wanted to slow down and make it last. It was just…that look in her eyes; God, that look drove him out of his mind! That and the way her sweet little cunt spasmed all around him—he couldn't get deep enough. He couldn't get enough, period. He doubted he ever would.

"What the fuck are you doing to me?" The question was rhetorical, one he didn't really expect an answer for.

Since when had that ever stopped her, though? He got one, anyway.

"I'm loving you."

Shit, shit, shit! He was going to come. Too soon! Way too fucking soon. But he could feel it building to the point of no return; his testicles were close to exploding no matter what he did. And there was just no way in hell he was going to pull out now. He couldn't. Her pussy sucked him in, demanding what he was giving her. Legs locked around his waist weren't going to let him go, and he didn't want them to.

He had to shift so he could hold her wrists with one hand, then he reached between them to work her clit, rubbing mercilessly on the nub until she was sobbing, bucking every bit as wildly as he was.

"That's right, baby. Come for me." Because he couldn't hold back. There was nothing more important right now than exploding inside her channel.

"Oh, God, Azriel!"

Her pussy convulsed, clenching down on him tight, so fucking tight. He let go of her hands, loving the way her nails raked down his back, the way her little teeth sank into his shoulder.

"Fuck, baby!" His climax started at the base of his spine, erupting from the depths of his very soul.

He was lost. Caught up in the whirlwind that was Michelene. It seemed as if he were frozen rigid inside her for all eternity before he collapsed beside her. On reflex, he gathered her in, tucking her tight into his side. His body just didn't like to be separate from hers.

It should've been enough. His body was sated, and she had been satisfied. Until the next time he needed her, that should've been enough. But his mouth opened, and it completely shocked the shit out of him when he heard the words uttered in his own voice.

"I love you so damn much." And he meant it.

What the fuck?

CHAPTER 14

Azriel had been in such a good mood. Apparently Michelene loved the idea of boutiques coming to her rather than going to them. And they only brought her size, which she declared was so much more convenient. Who knew it could be so amusing watching her pick frilly little things that caught her fancy? The unbridled joy on her face just made him feel all… Fuck, he was that guy. The entire time she'd tried on different outfits he'd mentally pictured each place he would take her to suit that outfit. Pussy whipped. Totally and completely fucking gone.

Right now she was passed out, wearing a delightful little white baby doll teddy. Damn, but she looked adorable in that thing. How was a man supposed to resist? Of course the matching panties had to go, but there was something to be said about lace on skin. Essential parts tended to peek through the openings in the woven material, making it ever so easy to get a taste. The three hours of watching her pick out a new wardrobe were oh so worth it when they were followed by three hours of his baby girl showing him how grateful she was.

Then this call had come. Finding out the identity of Michelene's stalker was important to him—aside from taking care of the problem of her mother, it was paramount. The last thing he'd expected was for her problems to be so closely entangled in his own. So now it was back to business. This shit had to be ended soon. Not only the threat against Michelene, but the insane family drama that caused those dark shadows in her eyes. He wouldn't tolerate them anymore.

"Father Emmanuel Cruz. First cousin to one Rico Cruz, who I hear is none too pleased about you declining a contract." Pierre Cadeau told him. Michelene's brother was a wild card, but one she believed had no hand in her problems, so Azriel had reached out to him to accomplish this task.

"You're sure?" But even as Azriel asked, he knew the answer. Not used to working with anyone, he had set about finding out some information for himself. He just wanted to see how much this man knew and how much he was willing to share.

"I have a vested interest in being absolutely positive." The reply was dry. Almost casual. Azriel wasn't fooled in the least. There was anger, irritation and more than a little curiosity behind those words. Unless he was mistaken, which was rare, there was even a little bit of a threat. Not an outward challenge, just an underlying menace.

Normally Azriel would be offended. Not today. For one thing he knew far more about Pierre than he had known about any of his marks. Mostly he was just curious. However, being curious didn't make him stupid. Casting a quick glance at the stairway leading to the bedroom, he quickly strode to his office, locking himself behind the soundproof door. Having a completely soundproof office was a little bit of overkill given he'd always existed alone. Now he was thankful for it. There were questions that needed to be answered, and he was finding that with anything to do with Michelene it was best he asked them.

"Have you been looking for your sister in order to kill her or have her harmed in any way?" Because really, that would mean life or death for this man. Michelene might trust Pierre Cadeau, but Azriel didn't. He didn't trust anyone but himself with her safety. "I hear that your mother is talking of Michelene taking her place one day. That has to upset you."

"My sister is no threat to me. She doesn't want

anything to do with the family business. And even if she did, she would have no reason to fear me. My mother is a lying bitch." Well, it seemed that Pierre wasn't one to mince words. "I would never trust my mother with my sister's safety."

"Took a while to come to that conclusion, did it not?" It was fine to say that now, but where had this man been most of Michelene's life? Azriel already knew she wanted nothing to do with what her mother and brother did for a living. Just like he knew part of Pierre's failings. In his book, because her brother had failed to protect her, he was unfit. Period.

"Had I known I would've killed May myself," Pierre spit out at him through the phone. "I should've been there. I wasn't. I am rectifying that now. If Michelene wants to collect the debt she owes from me, I will be the last one to stop her."

"And now?" Azriel pressed. "Is there a reason why your mother is still living?" Yeah, he knew he was pressing buttons most people didn't like pressed, but he wasn't one to go into any situation blind.

"May is Michelene's to kill unless she tells me otherwise," Pierre responded smoothly. "Had she succeeded in killing May the first time, my life would be infinitely easier, but you knew that already. If I thought for a second she was in danger with you I would have retrieved her by now. And yeah, I know where you are. My sister appears happy. I am content for now. But should that change, you and I might have a problem."

Azriel had to smile at that. He had been very well aware several of the delivery boys who dropped off food from time to time were anything but delivery boys. Their eyes were a little too interested, taking in as much as they could in the brief time they were at the door.

"But it's been a few days since you've been able to have one of your spies in our home." Cause, yeah, once or twice he could understand to ease a brother's worried mind. He'd read somewhere familial bonds were often strong and all that. But given what Azriel knew of their mother, there was no way he would allow it more than a few times. Did this man really believe he was dealing with some street thug?

"I expected nothing less." Pierre chuckled. "But I had to at least try. You do understand that, right?"

Any more would probably be beating a dead horse, so Azriel swiftly changed subjects. While May Brown was admittedly a greater threat than this crazed stalker priest, Azriel needed to be prepared on all sides. That the priest was related to the drug lord was quite the coincidence, and Azriel didn't believe in coincidences.

"I need to know everything there is to know about this Father Cruz," Azriel told him. In order to eliminate the enemy, it was always wise to find out the most one could about him. Nothing he had researched about the Cruz Cartel ever mentioned a priest for a cousin. But then, why would it? "I will take care of Rico myself."

The thought of Michelene being sold to Rico Cruz made his stomach turn. He would make sure the man was utterly destroyed just for having the balls to think he could purchase a woman like her. One day man might learn you couldn't just buy the rare things in life. Some you had to work for; others were just destiny.

"Then you should know Michelene knew him as a child."

Azriel didn't like the way Pierre said that. "What do you mean knew him?" Yet another question that really needed to be asked. But he didn't want to know the answer.

"He was our father's…personal priest." Pierre was leaving a lot unsaid. The hesitation in his voice, the underlying rage. "That is Michie's story to tell. But I will find out where's he been and what he's been doing since then. If you want to know specifics about that time, ask Michie. If she doesn't tell you, leave it alone." Pierre was resolute, Azriel could tell.

Well, shit. Just when their relationship, such as it was,

had stabilized a bit, he was going to have to piss her off. Azriel hated pissing Michelene off. In fact, he was pretty sure he hated Pierre right about now. He was going to have to tread very carefully around this subject. She had a tendency to shut down when he pushed too much about her childhood.

Because Michelene had spoken of her brother with nothing but affection, Azriel had decided to include him in his plans. God, it went against the grain to work with anyone else, especially someone with so many ties. Ties were messy. But with all she'd told him, he'd decided to trust the man with a few small tasks, like clearing out her apartment and finding out who had been following her. That had paid off, but that didn't mean he trusted the man fully.

"Are you sure your mother doesn't know anything about my whereabouts? She's known to have ears everywhere." That was a test. No, May Brown didn't have a clue where her daughter was. Though Azriel kept his circles small and tight, he wasn't without resources of his own. The entire time he had "entrusted" Pierre with a few small tasks, he had eyes and ears on everything the man did. And on Madam Brown.

"I am positive," Pierre stated. "But I am sure your spies told you that."

Good man. Maybe they'd get along after all. As long as it wasn't too close. "We will need to meet to finalize our plans. I will get back to you with a time and place."

With that Azriel ended the call and began composing a detailed list of competitors and allies of the Cruz Cartel. There was no doubt in his mind Cruz was assisting his cousin in some way. Whether it was to get back at him for refusing the contract or taking the woman he'd thought to have as his own was of no consequence. Cruz would never be good enough for Michelene and assisting in a petty turf war was something Azriel just didn't do. It was messy and came with repercussions, always biting you in the ass on the back end. It was ironic, though, that the very person Cruz had wanted to have killed was none other than Madam May Brown. He idly wondered if she had a clue her main source in Columbia wanted her dead.

Cruz's friends and associates would soon know. The drug lord had done the one thing that would surely be the end of him—he had pissed Azriel off. The emotionless killing machine now had a very real stake in seeing the man's empire crumble to nothingness. The beauty of it was, Azriel wouldn't be the one to destroy him. Cruz had done that himself. All Azriel had to do was set a chain of events in motion and it was over for Cruz. There were more than a few Colombian politicians more than happy with Azriel's past service, more than one U.S. federal agent looking to make their bones, and there were always other cartels looking to make inroads.

There would be a bloodbath in the end, and bloodbaths were what Azriel did the best.

CHAPTER 15

"Tell me about Father Emmanuel."

Michelene froze, the glass of wine she'd been about to drink from suspended in midair. She could feel the tension in the delicate crystal wineglass she held, but it was so hard to loosen her grip. Suddenly she felt cold, exposed in a room full of elegant strangers. The opportunity for a night out seemed like a dream come true after weeks closed off in Azriel's apartment. Now she just wanted to go back, jump under the covers and hide. Maybe if she hid long enough the question would just fade away. She didn't want to even think about the answer. Or maybe she could make a run for it, haul ass out of the restaurant and never look back.

Looking at Azriel was a mistake. He was as he always was. On the surface, calm, collected, waiting. Underneath she could see a swirl of emotions through the windows of his eyes. He was seething; she should have seen that before now. She'd been so caught up in the excitement of going out, she hadn't sensed his underlying mood. There was no way that much anger hadn't been there before now. Although she knew full well he wasn't mad at her, she hated seeing that rage. She knew the cause, and that made it awful. Worse than awful.

"You know..." Setting the glass down, she tried a bright smile. One she knew she failed at miserably, but she couldn't fake casual indifference right now. But she could fake being happy like nobody's business. A trait she'd picked up so very long ago. "...the play tonight was a first for me."

Not for a second did she believe Azriel would allow her to get away with deflecting. It was merely to give herself some time. The last thing she'd ever intended to do was to tell him about this part of her life. The things her mother had done were one thing. Not only were those memories too fresh, but she had been able to exact some sort of vengeance for that. And she would eventually be able to collect the ultimate retribution. The earlier stuff... It was just too pathetic. Nothing could change it; there would be no revenge for it. She neither wanted nor needed that kind of pity from him. And he would pity her. She had seen it in Pierre's eyes every time he looked at her. She didn't want to look at Azriel and see the same.

"I'm aware of this." Azriel looked patient. His tone sounded patient. But she knew he was anything but. It was all in those silvery eyes narrowed into slits as well as the tic. Generally she loved seeing it. Not so much right now. "Tell me what I want to know, Michelene."

Squirming in her seat, she looked around at all the people sitting so comfortably, engaged in quiet conversations. How oblivious they all appeared to be, completely unaware of the very real ugliness outside their beautiful world. Were any of them secretly listening in? Had any of them spotted the imposters in their midst? Because this world, the one where people wore fancy, sparkling clothes to a restaurant that didn't include prices on the menu, ignored the world she and Azriel hailed from. They denied the existence of those less fortunate or desperate and pretended lives like hers only happened in movies. She thought she could pretend to be one of them, just for tonight, then he had to go and bring up the worst time of her life.

"I can't." Looking anywhere but at him, she fought back hot tears she never allowed herself to shed. Shame surrounded her like a shroud, cutting off the air. God, how she hated this weakness. "Not here."

There was no reply. It was one of those rare times when she had no idea what to expect from him. The silence stretched for what seemed like forever. Tension wound her body up so tight she was afraid she would snap. Finally she had no choice but to look up at him, which was what he was waiting for.

He knew. She knew he knew. Yet there was no pity there to be seen. Just a softness that damn near broke her.

"Eat your food. You're going to need your strength."

Damn.

***

She was afraid to tell him. That pissed him off, even if he could logically understand her fear. It was just that, damn it, she should know better by now. She should know him. Granted they had only known one another for a little over a month, but in that time they'd shared more than most couples do in a lifetime. Azriel had let her in—something he'd never done with anyone else. From the start there had always been this connection between them, something…different. This was no boy-meet-girl bullshit. The bond was as immediate as it was unbreakable. Nothing, no one would ever keep them apart. Hadn't he admitted she felt his presence long before he'd made himself known? Why couldn't she feel him now?

The reason he was pushing her now was because she

really needed to let this out. Over the years she had placed the distant past in some dark corner of her soul, thinking herself safe from it. Because danger was always present, she had been able to push it away; there had always been too much at hand to deal with. But bits and pieces were bound to leak out over time, and when they did, they would slowly poison her. He'd seen it happen repeatedly to otherwise stable people. It was something he would not and could not allow. All of her belonged to him; therefore all of her was in his care. He would do anything and everything within his power and beyond to ensure her complete wellbeing. That mean being more than a shield against her enemies. He had to shield her against herself too.

Watching while she played with her food was hellish. The demons that haunted her lurked behind every false smile she threw his way. Enduring it was all he could do. There'd been times where he'd cased a mark for weeks, waiting for an opportunity to get close and never felt this kind of agitation. Crawling out of his own skin would be easier than this. Finally, she managed to choke down at least half of what had been on her plate. Great.

By the time he was able to hustle her out of the restaurant and into the waiting car he was at the very end of his patience. Concentrating on the dark streets outside the car window, he had to bite the inside of his cheek to keep himself in check. Thank God he had thought to get a driver. He might've broken the land-speed record getting her home.

"Take off your clothes," he ordered as soon as he hustled her inside the apartment. A plan had come to mind on the way here. It was the only thing he could think of to make sure she didn't try to hide from him. Nude, she seemed far freer, more open. Besides, it was symbolic, a way to symbolize nothing was to be kept from him.

Leaving her where she stood he went about checking security and setting the specialized alarms he'd had installed. He heard rather than saw her move toward the staircase, obviously heading up to the bedroom.

"No." He stopped her cold. "Here. You will undress here. Now."

He didn't watch. He couldn't just yet. He already knew there was indecision stamped all over her face as she debated whether or not to obey him. The little imp knew how to push him, twist him up in knots before turning him inside out in a way that only a fully grown woman could. But that didn't mean he couldn't see the vulnerable little girl inside her. Frankly, he didn't know if he was strong enough to handle watching that part of her right now. It was going to take a few seconds for him to steel himself and his resolve.

Sitting down in a large leather armchair, he trained his gaze to the windows for a few moments before looking back to her. Standing in only her lingerie, Michelene looked at him as if he were the big bad wolf, her dress and shoes in a little pile by her feet. At least she wasn't trying to cover herself. Biting her bottom lip, she just stood there fidgeting. He almost had to smile at that.

"Are you unclear about what I told you to do?" Raising his brow, he placed his arms on the chair, his hands digging into the leather. God damn, he just wanted to gather her in his arms and kiss all that insecurity away. But he couldn't do that.

"Why do I have to be naked to have a conversation?" Ahhh, there was his little brat. Chin raised, she was all defiance and sass. The sadness was still there, and the guilt. Guilt that wasn't hers to carry.

Which was why he had to go through with this.

"There isn't going to be a conversation." He kept his tone neutral. He would brook no argument in this. You will tell me what I want to know—what I need to know."

"I don't need to be nude to speak." Gaining confidence, her hands went to her hips, glossy lips all pouty and kissable. It was enchanting, but it wasn't changing his mind. "And you don't need to know about…about my childhood."

This could go on forever unless he put a stop to it.

"Come here, Michelene." Gone were any traces of amusement he might've shown previously, because all amusement was gone. He was done arguing. Still, it was more than a little gratifying to see her do as she was told.

As soon as she was in grabbing distance, he had her over his knees, the palm of his hand crashing down on the cheeks of her ample, supple ass. No, his ample, supple ass. Fuck, did this feel good. Spanking her was just a way to show her he was serious about her wellbeing, that he would accept no argument when he was doing something that could only help her. Plus, it felt really fucking good! Damned if her hips didn't rise to meet his swings. There were no loud cries or protestations. Just low moans that made his cock jerk, throbbing to be inside her. Too bad it was going to have to wait.

"Up." He helped her as he ordered her. Her legs were just a little bit on the shaky side.

There were tears streaming down her cheeks, but he knew he hadn't really hurt her. He could never do that. Just a sting of pain was all she needed.

"Clothes. Off." This time she didn't hesitate. Bra and panties were off in a heartbeat. "Good girl."

The tentative smile on her lips almost made him

reconsider. But not quite.

"Kneel beside me and tell what I want to know."

He didn't have to ask again.

CHAPTER 16

"My mother never had much of a maternal instinct." Michelene held her head down. She didn't really have a reason for doing it; nothing she said would make Azriel turn away from her. She just—the pity in Pierre's eyes had always infuriated her, and shamed her. It would kill her to have Azriel look at her that way. But he would not be denied. "When I was very little, she left Pierre and me with our father. I used to think she just didn't know about my father, about what he liked…"

"And was that, Michelene?" Azriel startled her by asking.

Right. When she trailed off, she'd stopped talking altogether. Without realizing it, her mind had immediately begun searching for the right words to gloss it all over. Little euphemisms that would say it without her having to give voice to it. Whenever her thoughts drifted to that black, dank corner of her memory she glossed over it to herself. Why did she do that?

"My father was a pedophile." She surprised herself by looking directly into his gaze as she spat out the words. Like she was daring him. Maybe in a way she was. So she pushed, just to test him. Let's see if he could still look at her without feeling sorry for herself. "I was his favorite, you know. Even though he had boatloads of girls at least once a month, he would always sneak into my room when the help or Pierre weren't around. And he always found places to send Pierre off to." Still not pity. No anything. He just watched her silently, and for the first time, his eyes were completely void of emotion.

"Continue."

Damn it, she'd stopped talking again.

"He always felt guilty afterwards. There was a priest who lived with us then. Father Emmanuel. I know damn well they shared girls sometimes, when there was some poor kid that caught my father's eye. But he would still confess to that bastard anyway. Like one sick freak could absolve the other. He—Father Emmanuel—would make me confess for tempting my father. But because I was a 'daughter of Lilith,' I had to do so nude. On my knees. Like right now."

"Is that supposed to make me feel guilty, Michelene?" God, did he have to sound so gentle, so freaking understanding when he said that?

"No." Yeah, she had totally said it on purpose. It was true, but she'd punctuated every word so she could make him feel bad.

Thank God it hadn't worked. And he still didn't look like he pitied her. He looked...proud.

"Yes, you did. But I forgive you. This time. Continue. And no interruptions this time."

Swallowing the lump in her throat, she had to take a deep breath before going on.

"He never touched me—Father Emmanuel, I mean. He would look at me like he wanted to, but he never even tried. Maybe my father threatened him. I don't know. I hated them both. I wanted to kill them both. But the night my father died, the priest took his body somewhere, and I never saw him again."

Damn, that felt good! It was like she had been released from something that had been weighing her down. Partially, anyway. There was more.

"How did your father die?" Azriel pressed in a quiet, but firm voice.

How could he have possibly known? Their gazes collided and held; she couldn't look away. She couldn't lie.

And there was no way he was going to let her get away with not answering.

"I killed him." No one except Pierre and Father Emmanuel knew that for sure. Now Azriel knew what she'd never dared to even think about too long. "Pierre walked in on a confession. I don't know how much he heard, but he lost it. He attacked my father with a knife, but the priest was there to help him. I just sat there crying. My father beat Pierre pretty bad. He was only ten. There wasn't much he could do against two grown men."

"I'm not interested in excuses for your brother, Michelene." Azriel cut her off as she babbled on in her brother's defense.

"He has nothing to be excused for!" she shot back. Naked and on her knees she might be, but Pierre wasn't at fault here, and she wasn't going to allow Azriel to blame him.

"So you say." He was completely unfazed by her outburst. "Tell me how your father died."

"I slit his throat." There. She said it. "Pierre was hurt pretty bad, but he gave me a switchblade the very next morning, teaching me how to use it. He told me if my father ever came into my room again, I should wait for the right moment and cut him across the jugular. That very night I killed him. I didn't just cut his throat, I stabbed him repeatedly, screaming. That's how Father Emmanuel found me. He cleaned me up and told me to go sleep in Pierre's room. The next morning my mother was back, my room was clean and my father was just gone. My mother acted like it never happened. So I did too." She shrugged. "The only person I ever told was Pierre. How did you know?"

"I guessed."

Wow, was she really that transparent?

"Yeah, well at least my mother waited until after puberty before she dangled me in front of men she wanted to make alliances with. I was seventeen before she made me whore for the good of the family business. I got tired of it. So when she tried to sell me off permanently, I tried to do the same thing to her that I did to my father. I even used the same switchblade. Then I ran. I should've waited. I should've made sure she was dead…"

There was nothing left. The whole thing, telling it from beginning to end, was exhausting. She wanted to cry; she wanted to sleep—hell, she had no idea what she wanted.

"Two more questions." Azriel guided her head down to his knee, then began to stroke her hair. It felt sublime, that simple caress. She felt cherished, all from this small act. "Why didn't you go to your brother when you mother informed you she'd arranged a marriage for you? And are you very sure you want to be the one who kills her?"

Not "Are you sure you want her dead?" but "Are you sure you want to be the one that kills her?" God, she loved this man so much!

"Pierre was in the Middle East. She always timed things like that," she mumbled against the fine linen of his slacks. Damn, she felt drained. None of it mattered anymore. Not her father or her mother. "I had no way to contact him. She saw to that. Even if I called, he wouldn't have made it home in time. I never told him about May because he would've killed her in a fit of rage. That would've been disastrous for him. And yes, I want to kill her. It is my right."

"Then you will." So simple. So straightforward. There was no doubt in her mind he would make it happen. "Come." All he had to do was pat his lap and she was there, nestled against his solid chest, snuggling in the stalwart arms that held her. "Father Emmanuel was the man stalking you. Now I have a good idea why. I will take care of him, and I will deliver your mother to you."

Yes, he would. Because taking care of her was what he did.

***

Azriel didn't move for well over an hour. Holding Michelene as she slept, he thought it best not to move lest he wake her up. Tonight had drained her, but he believed it was all for the best. Now there was nothing between them. She would never know how much her words had torn him apart. For years he'd taken contracts, uncaring about who he was killing or why. All the while there were people like her parents, and that sick-ass priest who really needed killing. Perhaps it was time to reevaluate his life choices. Later, of course, after this mess was cleaned up.

He hated to put her to bed, but eventually he had to. As much as he wanted to strip and crawl into bed with her, he quietly made his way back downstairs, walking past the little pile of clothes in the front room. Secretly he loved finding frilly, girly, pastel things all over the place. As well as the personal touches here and there. It made the place feel warmer. Like a home.

Shit, he was seriously turning into that guy. He was practically making himself sick. If only it didn't feel so good.

With a rueful smile, he locked himself in his office and called Pierre.

"Spread the word in all the right places I'll be at my beach house this weekend," he told him quickly. He needed to get upstairs to his woman before she woke up. "Make sure Cruz's people as well as your mother's know. I want them all there."

"I'll be there too," Pierre insisted. There was enough conviction on his voice that Azriel didn't waste his time arguing. "I'll be bringing backup."

"As you wish." This could potentially get messy. Azriel made a mental note to set up airtight alibis for Michelene and himself. "But your mother is Michelene's to deal with as she wishes. The priest is all mine."

But first, he was going to make him suffer.

CHAPTER 17

The room was pitch dark when she woke. Azriel must've darkened the windows. He did that when he didn't want anything to wake her. It made no difference; she didn't need the light. His body was curled around hers, completely surrounding her with hard, male flesh. At first she just lay there, trying to figure out how she felt. There was an avalanche of emotions sweeping over her.

Peace. Security. Sadness.

And that rock-solid erection poking her in the backside was heating her blood at a rapid rate. Steady, rhythmic breathing behind her told her Azriel was asleep, but he was a really light sleeper.

Not so subtly she pressed back against him, using the cheeks of her ass to gently massage his cock. The wetness of precum gradually leaked onto her skin, giving her natural lubrication. Noting the change in his breathing, she began moving more aggressively, increasing her speed until she couldn't stand it. She needed him.

"Azriel?" Why didn't he take her? Generally when she teased him like this, he'd have her flipped over, dick deep inside her in seconds.

"Yes?" He wasn't unaffected. There was a deep huskiness to his voice. That sexy drawl he got when he wanted her.

"Are you going to do anything?" She still hadn't stopped moving. This agonizing hunger wouldn't go away until he took her. Fucked her. Made her scream.

"I am doing something. I am lying next to you."

Shit! She hated it when he got like this. Obstinate for the sake of being obstinate.

"Please fuck me." Sometimes he just liked to make her say it. It was a hell of a lot easier to say it now. Those words had been so foreign to her in the beginning he had practically had to force them out of her. "I need you."

Bad. Only he could relieve the fervent hunger centered deep inside her pussy.

"I'm right here, baby." Rolling on his back, he casually placed his hands behind his head. "All yours."

Wow, he really wasn't going to do anything. That engorged cock was at attention, bobbing in the air as if it could sense her hunger. The little helmet at the tip glistened with proof he wanted her every bit as much as she wanted him. So why wasn't he doing anything about it?

"Don't you want me?" He did, she knew it. But his behavior was baffling. What exactly was he trying to prove?

"You know better," he chided as if he had been inside her thoughts. But he didn't move.

Urgh! The man was really trying to drive her insane.

"Michelene, I'm here. I'm not going anywhere. If you want something, take it. I won't stop you. I have every intention of loving every second."

Indecision held her in place. In their time together she'd never been the one to initiate sex. Azriel had always been in complete control. She wasn't sure if she could do this. Looking at him sprawled on the bed, waiting, watching her, he'd never looked more inviting to her. Reaching out, she ran her hand slowly across his chiseled chest. It was so odd how it felt so firm, yet so smooth. She could just make out little changes on his face as her hands moved lower to his pelvis, then even lower to cup his testicles. They were heavy, wrinkly but so very soft.

Just to experiment a little, she began to play with them. Just a little massage, a slight squeeze.

"Careful, baby," he groaned, but didn't make a move to

stop her. "They're fragile."

Reluctantly she let them fall from her hands, moving on to his shaft. So wonderfully long, beautifully thick and hard. When she squeezed it, his face contorted instantly in a picture of anguished need. She felt an immediate, corresponding reaction deep in her gut. Gathering confidence, she began to move, stroking him up and down. She loved the way he felt. It was so stiff, so sleek. She could feel the veins straining against his skin. His hips moved but he otherwise stayed exactly where he was.

Okay, then.

Leaning over his large frame, she trailed kisses across his chest while she worked him. Oh, God, the way he moaned made the wetness in her pussy so much worse. Was there anything in the world sexier than the dark rumble of a man experiencing pleasure? Keeping one hand on his cock, she raked her nails across his chest while she bit him hard on his shoulder, just because she could.

That got a reaction. His body bucked, his hand flying out to grasp her hair in a punishing hold. Air hissed through his teeth, but he didn't try to push her away.

"Keep teasing me and you're going to get another spanking, little girl."

She had to smile at the gruff warning. That was what she was counting on.

"I'm not a little girl." She pouted, finally releasing his cock before sliding her body up his to lie on top of him fully.

"Prove it," he challenged.

That was a dare she decided to take him up on, gladly.

Straddling him, she couldn't resist sliding her dewy pussy up the length of his dick, teasing the head at the opening just a little. That look! The furious glare he gave her, so full of promises of payback. This was turning out to be a hell of a lot more fun than she'd thought. Canting her hips, she positioned him at her opening, then dropped down, forgetting to consider the length and girth of his shaft.

The breath left her lungs in a whoosh. Fuck, she couldn't move, couldn't draw in enough air! The burn was intense, stretching her more fully than when he took her from behind.

"It's okay, baby. Just breathe. Breathe for me, sweetheart."

The hands rubbing up her thighs, across her lower back, prompted her body to relax. The burn in her pussy perceptibly evolved from the almost too painful sting to pure liquid heat. She felt her channel flooding, adding the moisture she needed to move. Even if it hadn't been so, she was helpless to do anything but move.

The friction was exquisite, relieving the ache, yet building the overall need. She could feel him, his dick gently pulsating inside her, jerking every so often as she slid her slippery inner walls up and down in a deliberate rhythm. Every nerve ending in her channel was alive, firing off tiny bubbles of delight inside her. Azriel grasped her hips, but refrained from attempting to guide her movements. Jaw set, his eyes blazed up at her, silently urging her on. Every time she paused that tic appeared, beads of sweat popping out all over his brow.

This was her doing; she was creating that wild, desperate look. Licking her lips, she braced her hands on his shoulders, sank all the way down on him, then swiveled her hips in a slow, circular motion. Holy fuck, that felt marvelously fantastic! The head of his cock hit something inside, deeper than her g-spot. Or maybe it more fully hit it. She didn't have a clue and didn't care. It felt too good to care about anything. She couldn't stop the motion. Every twist caused his cockhead to press that spot, building and building until her body shook with an internal explosion so intense she screamed.

"Good girl," Azriel purred at her. "But you're not done."

***

It had taken everything within him to allow her to

explore his body to her heart's content. Fuck, when she dropped that hot little pussy down on him, he wanted to do nothing less than flip her and pile-drive inside over and over again until she forgot her own name. This had been for her, so that she could be in control of her body, her pleasure.

Now it was time to remind her of the pleasure he could bring her when he was in charge. It was so easy to lift them both so they remained connected. Kneeling in the middle of the bed, he kept her seated on his lap, but was fully able to thrust up inside her.

"Ride with me, baby," he growled, forcing her down on him as he powered up. "Show me what a good girl you are."

So god damn beautiful. Fuck, he needed to kiss her. Her lips, her forehead, her neck. Anyplace his mouth could reach. The liquid-velvet pussy contracted at his words. She loved to be called his "good girl." And shit, that throbbing inside her cunt was heaven. Sweat coated their bodies; rough animalistic grunts filled the air. Yet he wanted more. He wanted her to know to whom she now belonged. There could be no doubt she was his. The drive to make an indelible mark on her very soul was primal and could not be denied.

Bending her body slightly backward, his mouth swept

down to her breast. Sucking insistently on a nipple, he pounded her mercilessly. Her breasts were ultrasensitive, he knew through hours of exploration. As he intended, her pussy began to spasm, hard. Heaven or hell, he wasn't sure which, but he knew all too well she'd gotten under his skin. She was in his fucking blood. One smile and she could drive him out of his mind.

Copious amounts of her juices bathed his cock, yet she was still so damn tight. She was going to make him come, but he didn't want to stop. Never wanted to stop.

"Oh God! Oh God, Azriel!"

Fuck, yessss! There it was. Fingernails dug into his skin, perfect legs locked around his hips. The power of his orgasm rocked through him from his balls down to his toes. Clasping her body close against him, he erupted right along with her, pumping his very essence deep inside her.

"God, baby, I love you so fucking much," he managed to choke out, rubbing his cheek against hers. He loved her so fucking much he was trembling from it. "I'll never let anything hurt you ever again."

"I know," she sighed back at him. "That's why I love you."

CHAPTER 18

Five hours, thirty-seven minutes. This waiting shit was wearing his last nerve, and he was pretty damn sure he only had one left.

"Your book collection had a surprising number of works on the subject of psychopathy." Michelene shifted the hand lying on his lap, her cheek grazing the outline of his dick. She had one such book dangling in her hand.

Looking down at her lying on the couch like they didn't have a care in the world, Azriel had to smile. She was gorgeous. Wearing a lightweight white sundress, with the afternoon sun shining on her flawless skin, she looked almost otherworldly. He could see how a man might become obsessed with her. He damned sure was.

"I sought to understand myself better." Unwilling to keep anything from her, he answered honestly.

Five hours, forty minutes.

"People with a psychotic obsession are unable to control their need, whatever that need might be, according to this book by a Dr. Reginald Baker."

Azriel frowned. She was trying to tell him something. "And?"

"And, they will come," she said simply. "Father Emmanuel is obsessed with me for some unknowable reason. My mother is obsessed with control, power, and getting her way." Reaching up, her small hand caressed his cheek. A casual gesture of affection, but to him it felt precious. "They will come. And Pierre will come because he thinks he owes me something. Each of them is driven by an obsessive need of some kind, so they will come. Stop counting minutes."

All he could do was smile at that. His little miracle. Just like that, his body relaxed, tension flowing out of him as if it were being carried away by the tides outside. All it took was some simple casual touch, affection given so freely and honestly. And how quickly he'd come to need that from his bewitching mixture of woman, child, brat and minx. Everything about her was addicting. Now he finally understood why men would do anything for a woman. It was like he'd waited his entire life to be woken up by her kiss. And he should fucking hate being that sappy guy.

Instead he wondered how he had lived without this for so long.

"You are life to me." He hadn't meant to say those words, but it was true. She was the thing that kept him tethered to life. He'd never realized how disturbingly close he'd been to slipping into the darkness never to return.

"And you are everything to me." Sitting up as she said it, she straddled his lap and took his face between her hands. "You know that, right? You are more than I ever hoped to have, more than I could dream of. I love you, you know?"

"Yes, baby, I know." And it felt damn good. She felt so damn good.

Just as he was about to kiss her, the outer perimeter alarm went off.

***

Finally, she was there! Weeks scouring for any information he could find had led him back here, and at long last his diligence had paid off. Seth was so sure of himself, there weren't any guards outside the place, no hidden traps. It was so easy to sneak up close. The place may have had loads of floor-to-ceiling windows, especially the side facing the beach, but the side facing the road barely had any. There was a security system on the front door, but it wasn't as intricate as one would think a hit man would have. Emmanuel knew that because he'd already broken in to case the place several times before Seth's return. All he had to do now was avoid the few motion detectors along the long, curving driveway that led to the house from the road.

Easy enough. They reset automatically as soon as a small movement like those made by small animals faded. That was why he'd gotten a few frogs from a pet store. Working his way close he let a couple go at a time, then darted to just before the next set of sensors all the way to the door. He knew he wouldn't need Rico's men; that was why he'd ditched them over a hundred miles back. It'd been thoughtful of his cousin to provide the five rough-looking men, but he thought they might scare Michelene. Sneaking away from them had been child's play. They were probably looking for him even now.

His angel was in that house, and nothing was going to keep him from her. There was no way she was in there with Seth by choice. Never would he believe that. Oh, she may have looked content laying on the sofa with that monster. Emmanuel had watched for a while before he'd approached. Somehow Seth was controlling her, making her appear as if she was content. Michelene was a good girl; she'd always been biddable. Sooner or later she would've found a way to fight Seth, just like she'd fought her father. But this time, he would be brave and free her himself, like he should've done years ago.

How right his angel had been to baptize herself in the blood of that monster who had sired her. And she'd tried to do it again with that she-wolf of a mother. That proved she was righteous, pure. Even as a child she had eased his sickness because she was blessed, touched by heaven. God sent her to him to free him of those horrific demons that hounded him, made him do horrible things. It was destiny. The entire time he'd been her confessor, he hadn't felt the need to touch those tempting young vixens.

But then that bitch May had banished him from her. The urges returned even worse than before. For years, he had drowned in his sickness. With each passing year it had gotten worse. There was no way to fight it. Then out of nowhere he'd found her again. She'd walked right past him as he worked in a homeless shelter in that god-awful neighborhood. How he'd ached to take her right then! But he'd had no place to bring her. No place where they could be alone. There'd been no choice but to work for his cousin until he had enough money to make a place good enough for her. But Seth had stepped in right before he was ready. The hit man had ruined everything!

That was going to be set right today. It was hard not to giggle as he disabled the alarm. The passcode entry was so easy to bypass. Nothing so simple would keep him away now. So close. So very close.

***

Azriel Seth. What an amazing turn of events. Her little girl had captured herself quite an asset. May was positively giddy as she followed the poor, demented priest. To think she'd almost wasted what she thought was a worthless daughter on a Columbian drug lord just to ensure supply. But her daughter had proven herself to be far from worthless. Instead of the sweet, biddable simpleton May thought she had on her hands, she'd spawned a siren who'd lured a far greater asset into her web.

"Do you want us to go in with the freak?" One of her men interrupted her delicious daydreams.

What was his name? The man had been a quick replacement for Munoz, who'd disappeared without word or warning. Her son probably had a hand in that, but she couldn't be sure, and no one else seemed to know. Too bad this one wasn't as good in bed as Munoz had been. Probably the reason she couldn't remember his name.

"No." She didn't like to be questioned, but there were bigger matters at hand. "We'll wait for Seth to kill the irritating gnat. Twenty minutes should be about enough time." Eyes trained on the thin, demented priest slipping into the house, she started a mental countdown. Only a fool would think it was that easy to get the jump on a trained assassin. And there was no fool quite like a crazy fool. While Seth was busy with the priest, they would stroll right in and have a reasonable talk. Seth wanted her daughter? Well, then, he was going to have to give her his services exclusively. Otherwise, she'd snatch the little bitch out of his grasp. Now she knew the caliber of men she could lure with her daughter, there were a host of other men who'd probably give her a hell of a lot more than Rico Cruz.

Soon, May would have everything she was entitled to and the prospect of an heir much more easier to mold than her obstinate son. Her empire would expand, as well it should. Pierre would be livid when she informed him Michelene would be her second now, but the boy just couldn't be controlled. He never could, which was why he'd had to be sent away so much. Besides, as a female, how could she ever trust Pierre? Men were never to be trusted.

Maybe she wouldn't even punish Michelene for trying to knife her. Originally, she had planned on having the bitch taken down a peg or two, but if Seth agreed to her terms, she might overlook her daughter's past transgression. As much as May hated to admit it, Michelene had gained her respect. She hadn't seen the girl's potential. But she saw it very clearly now.

***

Almost all the players were in place. Pierre watched Father Emmanuel sneak into the house, watched his mother and the pathetically small group of men she'd brought with her. Both parties completely unaware they were waltzing into a trap. He had to admit, Azriel was a master at planning.

"Approach from the back of the house as soon as you see May's men move," he ordered his men via walkie talkie. He'd brought twenty-five hand-picked, battle-scarred men completely loyal to him. Unlike May, his men couldn't prove their loyalty by sleeping with him. They had to bleed for him. It would overwhelm the five May had brought. The five the priest had been supposed to have with him had been killed before they could leave the city.

"As soon as May is in the house, I want her men taken out," Pierre went on. "Don't go in unless I instruct you to."

It didn't matter that they were loyal, the fewer witnesses to what would go on inside, the better.

Seth would take care of the priest, but Pierre was determined to make damn sure May didn't get her claws on his sister. Although he'd sworn to Seth he would let Michelene take care of May, he was fully prepared to do it himself should the need arise. And of course it went without saying her man-whores were dead.

CHAPTER 19

Fear had been a constant for so long, it was easy for Michelene not to show it. Living in a world full of monsters, you couldn't show you were afraid. Especially when you're alone, and most of her life she'd been so very alone. With the few exceptions when Pierre was around, there had been no one to hide behind. Now she literally had an army of one. And her army allowed no fear. He may have been full of anticipatory tension before the first set of alarms went off, but at the sound of the small beeping signal, Azriel had been all business.

"LIE here on the sofa," he instructed, jumping to his feet with the grace of a jungle cat. He handed her a semi-automatic GP9, already loaded. "If he manages to get close, shoot him in the kneecaps, just like I told you. If I am not a few seconds behind, shoot him between the eyes, understand?"

Not waiting for her to answer, he slipped away on silent feet. Fear was there, but certainty overruled it. While it was appealing to curl up into a little ball and hide, it would do her no good. Pretending to be engrossed in the book she held, she concentrated on taking deep, calming breaths.

Soon, this would all be over and her life could really begin.

***

A crazed priest wasn't much of a challenge. The deluded man actually believed he'd bypassed Azriel's security alarms. Of course, Azriel'd gone to great lengths to make it appear that way. Even though he knew he wasn't dealing with a criminal mastermind, it was more than a little insulting the man actually believed it would be this easy to break into one of his homes. The beach house was exposed for the most part, so most of his alarms were buried under the sand. There were sensors under the driveway, cameras hidden in the shrubs. Azriel knew each time the priest had been in the house, he knew which room the man had been in, knew where May was, knew where her men were. Though he would take nothing for granted, it boggled his mind how impressed they both were at their own intelligence, when really they were being quite stupid.

Hugging the walls, Azriel crept toward where the priest would be. The priest was so focused on getting to Michelene, he didn't notice the amount of noise he was making. Nor was he checking the hallways he passed in his single-minded goal to get to the back sunroom where she waited. Slipping behind him was simple. Emmanuel didn't hear him, didn't sense him. In one quick strike, Azriel snatched a hand that was holding a syringe, pressing mercilessly inside the wrist until the priest's fingers let go. His opposite arm went around the much smaller man's throat, applying just the right amount of pressure. Too much and this would be over way too quickly. Azriel had no intention of letting him escape so easily. Emmanuel was unable to draw in enough air. In this cold, steady fashion, Azriel kept him immobile until the priest's body went lax. Just to be sure the loss of consciousness wasn't feigned, Azriel remained in that position a few moments more, though he eased the pressure on the priest's neck somewhat.

Finally, Azriel pulled out the ties he'd had in his pocket to secure the priest hand and foot. Heaving the thin man over his shoulder, he made his way back to Michelene. He calculated he had about fifteen minutes before May would come in. Then the fun could really begin.

***

There was no sound of gunshots, no sounds of a fight. Either Emmanuel had pulled off a major miracle or Seth had made quick work of him. There was just no scenario in which May could imagine the priest getting the upper hand, so Seth must've killed him. That was rather hot. Perhaps she might manage to get him to see the glories of a mature woman over the charms of her daughter.

"We're going in now," she snapped to her men, jumping out of the SUV. "All of you go around to the back. I'm going in the front." After all, she was just a concerned mother here to see about the wellbeing of her child. Seth had no reason to see her as a threat.

"By yourself?" The same bold man who'd questioned her earlier did it again now. What the hell was this man?

"I'm going through the front," May reiterated pointedly and forcefully. "I don't have any need of an escort, boy. I've been doing this kind of thing for a while." Besides, there was no danger. Not to her.

"I'm going with you," he stated mulishly.

Why did men always seem to think she needed their fucking protection? If anything, they should be protecting themselves against her.

"Fine." Although she smiled she was pissed. Later she would show this little worm who was in charge. No one contradicted her, especially in public. Now time was of the essence; she wouldn't be deterred by hired muscle who didn't know his place. Nothing could be allowed to get in the way of her goal.

"When I give you the signal, breach the house from the beach side. Make sure you see your indicators clearly," she snapped at the others, indicating the small black boxes each of them wore on a wristband. A small electronic signal that was soundless. Seth wouldn't have any warning. "Don't shoot unless you have to, and if you have to you better not hit my daughter."

With those final instructions, she turned and stomped toward the door, her mouthy muscle man in her wake.

***

He came awake slowly, his throat constricting painfully. It was hard to focus at first, but slowly his eyes began to adjust. His angel! She was right there, sitting demurely on the couch watching him. Though she was much older she still looked like the innocent eight-year-old he'd fallen in love with. Trying to rush forward to gather her in his arms, he found he couldn't move. Why couldn't he move?

"Michelene?" he croaked, trying to get his body to cooperate.

There was no memory of making it this far into the house, but he knew he was in the sunroom at the very back of the house. The waves could clearly be heard crashing to the shore behind him, and the sun shone directly into the room with zero barriers. It was almost blinding, that sunlight, but it framed her in a halo. That usually happened when he saw her; there always seemed to be a heavenly glow about her. How ethereal she looked all dressed in snow white to symbolize her purity. He knew she wouldn't let that animal corrupt her. She was too pure for that. Perfection, the way he'd always imagined.

Maybe he'd blacked out and he'd already had her in the place he prepared for her. That would explain why she looked so feminine. The sundress was so different from the drab colors she usually wore. It was something he might've picked out for her. Light and soft. The home he had for her was in Mexico, right on the beach far away from any town, any sign of corrupt civilization. Sometimes he lost time, moving on autopilot. But why couldn't he move?

And why was she looking at him like that? There was a disapproving frown on her face, and something in her eyes. Like she knew what he'd done to be free of the demons when he couldn't be close to her. Shame hit him in the chest. He would make it up to her. She would forgive him, and they would be perfect. They would come together and create a holy union, then become heavenly beings themselves.

"Don't you remember me?" That was it. She didn't recognize him. The years had aged him, he knew. He hadn't been able to eat much since that night she freed herself from her father. It would be all right now, though. Everything was going to be perfect. "I saved you. We can finally be together, finally be free. I would've never left you with that monster."

A bolt of lightning came from nowhere and slammed the left side of his temple. Pain exploded on that entire side of his face, scalding, blistering pain. Wetness trickled down to his chin, but he couldn't see what it was. HIs hand still refused to cooperate with the mental command to rise to wipe at it so he could see what it was. What was happening? None of the episodes he'd had in the past hurt from the outside. They started from within.

"M-m-m-Michelene!" It seemed as if his mouth was full of rocks. The room was starting to spin. He couldn't understand what was happening. "What—?"

CRACK!

The time the pain erupted from his chin, snapping his entire head backward with powerful force. A tooth flew from his mouth, and the sticky, metallic taste of his blood washed down his throat.

"So the paralytic does allow you to feel pain."

That voice! It was the sound of evil right above him. It was Seth! He'd never heard the man speak before, but that had to be how he sounded. Like death. But how was that possible? He'd had poison for the hit man. There'd been two syringes—one to keep Michelene calm and one to kill the man who'd tried to take her from him. Was Seth the reason why he couldn't remember anything? Had he found the syringe that had been in his pocket? The one he'd had in his hand had been lethal.

So he'd never made it to his angel. Somehow, Seth had stopped him. This couldn't be it. Evil couldn't triumph like this.

The view to his angel was blocked when Seth's big body stepped into his line of vision. Squatting down in front of him, Seth smiled. It was a horrible smile. One that promised pain, death, retribution.

"Did you really believe I would ever allow a sick fuck like you to take what is mine?" the devil asked softly. And Azriel was the devil. Satan incarnate looked him in the eyes. "Did you think you could just walk into my house and take my woman from right under my nose?"

Yes, that was exactly what he'd believed. Warm wetness bloomed from his crotch, the stale stench of urine permeating the air. Seth didn't bat an eyelash. Emmanuel knew he was facing his end. He should've brought his cousin's men, he should've planned better, thought through more angles—

CRACK!

A mighty fist slammed into his right eye. He hadn't even seen Seth move. The eye closed, the pain throbbing hard, going all the way to his brain.

So close! He had come so very close to the only thing he'd wanted for so long, he couldn't remember anything else. Now he was about to die, and Michelene would be lost to him forever. All he could do now was—

CRACK!

***

"May Brown, I presume?"

Having never seen Azriel Seth before, May hadn't been prepared for the beautiful man standing at the front door. Lethal, yes, but that was to be expected. There was an air about him that screamed "Don't fuck with me." That face could've been carved from stone; there was no emotion visible at all. The keen gray eyes looking at her dispassionately at her were lit with a knowledge she wasn't entirely comfortable with. A knowledge that shouldn't be in the eyes of a stranger.

"I see my daughter's been talking about me." What had Michelene told him? This man hated her. There were no outward signs of hatred, or much of any other emotion, but suddenly May was afraid. She couldn't remember being more so since she was a young girl.

Fingering the small electronic box in her pocket, she considered calling her men in now, but ultimately decided against it. This wasn't a man who'd respond kindly to a threat. Besides, there was still chance she could secure his exclusivity. Many of her enemies would shit their collective pants if she secured Azriel Seth. And Michelene had only defied her once; she wore that reminder on her skin. As long as she played nice, her daughter would do as she said, just as she'd always done.

"I take it Michelene is here?" she asked sweetly when he failed to respond to her little taunt. May knew she might not be as beautiful as her child, a fact that had always galled her, but she wasn't without her charm. She'd had her children very young, so she wasn't quite over the hill yet. Plus, she had more sex appeal than Michelene had ever had. The girl just didn't know how to use her assets to full advantage; at least, that was the way it used to be. Turning on her sex kitten to full blast, she gave him one of her best come-hither smiles, pushing her chest out to full advantage. Wearing a white linen suit with no shirt under the lightweight jack gave her plenty of cleavage, and her breasts were magnificent. "I've searched everywhere for her. She is my baby, you know. May I see her?"

There was a pointed stare at the pearls she wore around her neck to hide the scar her child had left her, then his gaze shifted to the muscles behind her.

"You are certainly in thick with the Cruz Cartel, aren't you?" Azriel confused her by asking.

What? What the ever-loving fuck?

The angel of death actually laughed at her. At her! "Oh, didn't you know your guard here is one of Rico Cruz's brothers?" Giving her a condescending grin, Seth actually scoffed at her. "He has eight. This one is one of the illegitimate ones, but very much a part of the inner circle. If you didn't know, I would hazard a guess that you've pissed Rico off. Or perhaps he's just here for his cousin, Father Emmanuel. But I am willing to bet, given he was the one to walk you to the door, he's here to pay me for the contract I originally declined."

"All of the above," muscle man responded while she gaped at both of them, talking as if she were the underling, the hired fucking help.

May repeatedly mashed down the button in a fury. Son of a bitch! This was all a setup. And she had walked right into it. She hadn't gotten this far by being this stupid. How had Cruz managed to get someone inside her organization? Pierre was going to pay for this shit. He was the idiot who'd found the man in the first place.

"In that case," Seth responded nonchalantly, stepping to the side, "do come in. Oh, and May? You're men won't be coming to your rescue. I'm afraid your son's men have sent them on to their eternal rest."

CHAPTER 20

Funny how the monsters of childhood looked so small and insignificant as an adult. Madam May Brown looked more like an aged doll trussed up in a chair next to the skeletal Father Emmanuel Cruz. The priest had passed out minutes before May had rang the doorbell, his face grotesquely swollen in shades of red, purple and blue. Michelene knew his chest and stomach area were probably the same shades. Azriel had given him quite the beat down, pounding the man over and over again, all without breaking a sweat or displaying any outward sign of the rage that was now evident all over the man's disfigured face.

Michelene was surprised to find she didn't feel anything for these two people besides disgust. Even the anger was gone in light of their current predicament. Maybe it was because she had Azriel on her side, but Michelene's fear was gone. Neither person would ever be in a position to hurt her again. Neither would live much longer.

"Let me do this, Michie," her brother pleaded, but handed her his prized machete nonetheless. "You don't need to do this."

Nothing could be further from the truth; she very much needed to do this. But how like Pierre to try to protect her when he couldn't. He'd always tried, but never was quite able to save her. She didn't blame him; it wasn't as if he didn't carry very real scars of his own.

"This is my battle." Smiling, she stepped into her brother's embrace. It took only a few moments before Azriel was there, gently removing her from Pierre's hug.

It was way over protective, but it made her smile, that warmth she always got whenever he did something like this spreading all over her body.

"She's my fucking sister," Pierre snarled at Azriel. "I'm nothing like my parents."

"She's my everything," Azriel responded calmly. "And no, you're not, but she is still mine."

"It's okay." Michelene laid a hand on her brother's chest, but quickly removed it at Azriel's low rumble of a growl. "Azriel is just very territorial, and I like it."

Pierre didn't smile back, but at least he didn't argue. That had to be a good sign.

"The priest is mine," Azriel announced, changing the charged atmosphere in the room to one of vengeance. Each of them there wanted it, but only she and her lover would extract it. He looked at the man who'd come in with her mother. "You can bring a part of him back to your family, but the body needs to be burned here in the house. I want him and May identified as Michelene and myself."

The man nodded, then gestured toward May. "The contract must be fulfilled."

How odd that Azriel had turned down the contract to kill her mother because he'd been more interested in getting to her. How ironic her mother would die with his assistance anyway.

"I told your brother no," Azriel said. "I meant it. I won't be the one killing May—Michelene will. You will pay her and tell your family it's done. I trust you have the money on you?"

"I do," the man affirmed. "As long as the bitch is dead and the fingers aren't pointed in our direction."

More than fingers would be pointed at the Cruz Cartel's direction. Tough luck for them all of this would be recorded, and it would be released after some creative editing. The family was about to find themselves in a world of hurt.

"Don't be stupid, Michelene!" May hissed, defiant to

the last. Michelene supposed it was brave in a way that the woman who'd given birth to her didn't even try to beg, wasn't attempting to bargain her way out. Instead she was counting on familial bonds to save her. That was just too funny. Instead of struggling against her bonds, she tried to negotiate. "I have powerful friends. You and your lover will be hunted. The last four years will look like child's play."

"Your friends are soon to become my friends." Pierre's voice was positively gleeful. "And I promise, my long-lost sister and I will stop at nothing to make no stone is unturned in finding your murderer."

The look that crossed May's face was almost comical. Disbelief, mixed with hatred with a healthy dose of fear thrown in. Reality had slammed home; there would be no saving herself.

"I'll haunt your fucking dreams," May hissed. "I promise you, my spirit won't leave you in peace."

"You've haunted my dreams for far too long." Michelene felt calm, centered. Pierre's machete no longer felt as heavy as it first had. "It's time I exorcised you."

"Wait! Michel—"

One swing. It only took one. The blade cut through the front of May's neck like a heated knife through butter, lodging in the bones in the back of her neck. May's eyes were wide with disbelief, an expression of pure terror forever etched on her face. Michelene was going to love remembering her mother like this. Azriel had to help her work the machete out of the bone. But it was all over. Done.

"Go sit down, baby," Azriel softly murmured, kissing her forehead. "I'll be with you in a moment."

There was blood on her dress. She loved this dress. There's no way she could take it to the cleaners. What an absurd thought to have given the circumstances.

It was all so surreal. Pierre threw a sheet over their mother's body. Did he think the sight would upset her? It didn't. Azriel was speaking in low, hushed tones to the Cruz man, but she couldn't make out what was being said. The man nodded, then handed her a thick manila envelope. She had no idea where it came from. Although she took it, she didn't bother opening it. There was no way she could look away from Azriel. Transfixed by the way he moved fluidly, almost like a dance. Slapping the priest awake, he set about slicing him with a KA-BAR, each time in a place that wouldn't kill the man. Leisurely he worked him over. When Emmanuel screamed as the knife pierced his flesh, Azriel would pause, waiting patiently until the screams subsided somewhat before starting again.

The Cruz man and Pierre simply waited, each of them

watching quietly as she did. Odd how no one in the room seemed at all fazed. With each slice, Michelene felt as if Azriel was cutting out the horrors of her childhood. The blood coating the man was washing away the degradation of her recent past. It was all so cleansing.

She had no idea how much time passed, but eventually, Azriel ran out of non-lethal places to cut. Instead of putting him immediately out of his misery, Azriel stabbed into his gut, twisted the knife, then yanked it out. Stepping back he watched as Emmanuel screamed, helpless to do anything as his life slowly ebbed away. All the while there was no visible expression on Azriel's face. He could've been carving a ham rather than a man.

The priest was near the end, the light in his eyes slowly fading. Still he managed to open his mouth to croak out his final statement of insanity.

"You could've saved me," he babbled through the blood sputtering from his mouth. "You calmed my need for—for younger girls. Only you could cure me. Only you."

Weird. All this time he seriously believed she was the cure for his sick desires?

His words, however, finally broke Azriel's mask. His face became picture of horrific fury.

"She belongs to me!" With what had to be superhuman

strength, Azriel buried his KA-BAR into the top of the man's skull.

EPILOGUE

There was a wild beauty about this place. The jungle came right up to the edge of civilization as if threatening to reclaim all of the land. The air was heavy with the perfume of exotic flowers, a constant threat of rain and the stench of third-world humanity. Michelene loved being out on the balcony at night. Besides, she had the perfect view of the Cruz compound, specifically Rico Cruz's study. It was fun watching the entire compound raided and looted by the Colombian army. Rico was barricaded in the study, staring at a gun in his shaking hands.

There was no way out for the poor bastard. Word was rampant he was behind the killing of Madam Brown. The brother who had actually been present at the beach house had been killed in a shootout with authorities at the Texas border, and more than thirty million in uncut cocaine had been seized. Buyers were out for blood. Underage whorehouses had been raided and closed down in four countries, all of their client lists in the hands of law enforcement…and newspapers. There were powerful politicians, crime bosses, millionaire sex tourists exposed by the failure of the Cruz family to guard their identities. The army was the least of Rico's worries.

Just as Rico put the gun to his mouth, she felt Azriel's presence behind her.

"You look sexy when you're all smug and self-satisfied."

Mmm, how good his arms felt around her.

"I'm finding vengeance makes me all hot and bothered." So did feeling his lips on her neck.

The night breeze caressed her bare thighs as Azriel slowly raised her dress up over her hips. Eyes closed, she concentrated on the sensation of soft cotton sliding up her skin, the air licking her thigh, her bare cunt. There were no panties to bar the path of his hands as they glided to the front of her pelvis, then dipped down to her pussy.

Oh God, his fingers never failed to drive her crazy when he toyed with her clit like that. Back arching, she opened her legs wider in invitation.

"You're not going to watch Rico work up the courage to pull the trigger?" he teased, nipping her ear playfully. "I think it's about to happen—the troops have made their way to the study door."

There was no way she could answer with words, not when he'd begun to enter her from behind. Shaking her head vigorously to indicate her answer, she bent forward, bracing her hands on the railing. What mattered right now wasn't whether or not Rico would take his own life. The only thing she cared about was the two of them together like this. The rest of the world simply didn't exist.

"Michelene?"

"Damn him! Why did he stop?

"I don't care if he blows his head off or not!" she pouted, pushing back against him. The friction was pure bliss.

"Why?" he insisted, pressing down hard on her clit.

Oh fuck, oh fuck she was seriously going to come, and they had barely started.

"Because he doesn't matter! Please, Azriel, I need you!"

But as usual, he wasn't to be deterred. "Why doesn't he matter?" he pushed, the pressure inside her growing ever stronger. The miniscule amount she was able to move by pushing her pussy back on his dick was not nearly enough. She needed more. And he knew it. "Tell me and I'll give you what you want; what you need."

"Because he can't hurt me!" Although she understood

he needed to know she trusted him to always protect her, now was a really rotten time to bring it up. "No one can hurt me. I have you."

"Good girl."

With that he slammed into inside her with ruthlessness that was her Azriel. And he was truly glorious.

The End

ABOUT THE AUTHOR

Shara is the first one to admit she is a little off. Her favorite movies are Steel Magnolias and Apocalypse Now, with a little Godfather and Animal House thrown in for fun. When not planning to take over the world, she can usually be found having deep and meaningful conversations with her kids about the meaning of life or trying to talk her husband into buying her weapons -- just in case of Armageddon.

You can drop Shara a line at: shara.azod@gmail.com
Or check her out at: www.sharaazod.com

Made in the USA
Charleston, SC
19 October 2015